oasis

round their way

D1565577

Published in 1996 by
INDEPENDENT MUSIC PRESS

British Library Cataloguing-in-Publication Data
A catalogue for this book is available from The British Library

ISBN 1-89-7783-10-8

All photographs courtesy of SIN: Photo credits: Plate 1: Peter Anderson,
George Bowstead, Steve Double; 2: Steve Double; 3: Piers Allaroyce; 4: Kim
Tonelli; 5: Peter Anderson, Kim Tonelli; 6: Peter Anderson, Andy Willsher;
7: Liane Hentscher; 8: Kim Tonelli

Independent Music Press
P.O.Box 3616, London
E2 9LN
On the Internet:
http://www.rise.co.uk/imp

oasis

round their way

by Mick Middles

Independent Music Press
London

CONTENTS

CHAPTER ONE
Looking Back In Anger

As if in rehearsal for the lead role of an amateur dramatic production of 'The King And I', Oasis singer Liam Gallagher is holding court, sitting in central supremacy in a darkened alcove in the chrome 'n' mirror interior of The Elizabethan pub in Heaton Moor, the Bohemian area of Stockport. It is Friday February 2, 1996, and the pub is filled, as usual, with uninhibited representatives of garishly clad local youth, parading around the bar, swilling lager and Hootch, falling into raucous conspiratorial huddles and generally 'tanking up' before surging 'down the hill', to the neon heaven of Coco Savannah's night-club in the town centre.

For most of the clientele, it seems strangely difficult not to find themselves staring in awe at the magnetic and familiar sun-glassed head of Gallagher, which bobs and bows conspicuously, deep in chatter and, no doubt, self-appraisal. Three girls, their figures tightly clasped in bright mini skirts, sashay to a post within groping distance of Gallagher and flash stocking clad legs and cleavages like the Cheddar Gorge in his direction. This rather appalling display is duly noted by Gallagher, and a mischievous grin spreads from ear to ear.

"I love it round 'ere, me," he is saying. "Heaton Moor, fucking love it, always wanted to live here...bought an 'ouse, I have!"

It is a comment one would normally associate with a particularly successful local car dealer, or insurance agent. Heaton Moor, for all its subtle attractions, and occasional splashes of glamour – a Simply Red manager lives less than 50 yards from the pub and various mildly successful local sportsmen and ex-Merseybeat bass players can often be seen waltzing into the newsagents – is hardly the Beverley Hills of the North. Neither is it a place where one might expect the singer from Oasis to aspire to, even if, within two weeks, his band would be topping the album charts in America after having already proven that they could outsell Michael Jackson and The Beatles in the UK.

Nevertheless the world had only recently opened up for Liam Gallagher, still only 22, still only a couple of years away from the dole queue, and still surrounded by the mates who gathered around him as he raged through the stark and savage streets of neighbouring Burnage during his teens. As a rock 'n' roll star, the tall, darkly bricked gothic detached homes, often split into decaying student flats that line the streets of Heaton Moor, might not seem so alluring. But as a cider quaffing teen, low on ambition, it must have seemed like pure heaven.

In February 1996, Liam Gallagher, unlike his older brother, Noel, who had decamped to Chelsea – a not altogether surprising move for one so steeped in the shadow of the sixties – was, if only temporarily, betwixt two extremes. It was well known in the area that he still enjoyed swaying drunkenly through the streets with his mates. It was, however, becoming increasingly difficult for him to enjoy himself in this way.

That night, as 'Roll With It' cranked up on The Elizabethan's jukebox, as the local girls hovered with predatory intent and as pockets of menace which could so easily turn against the resident celebrity built up inside the pub, it seemed obvious that Liam Gallagher's determination not to lose touch with his old world was already proving futile. He was striding the divide, armed, like his mentor and older brother, with the talent and the sheer unbridled confidence that had typified the astonishing and sudden rise of Oasis. Beneath that veneer, though, something rather less self-assured was surely lurking.

Margaret Gallagher – known locally, as 'Peggy' – 52-year-old-mother of the three Gallagher boys, Paul (30), Noel (28) and Liam, was only too well aware of the dangers that lurked behind the superstar status that two of her boys had recently attained. She sat in her semi-detached house, two miles away from Heaton Moor, in Burnage, partly relishing the lads' fantastic success, partly loathing it. For rarely would a day pass by without journalists, some of them having flown in from Europe, America and Japan, tapping on the door, requesting an exclusive audience.

Mostly they were briskly turned away by Paul. This was not an easy task, however, for the unassuming Peggy Gallagher. She had noticed also that simple pleasures, like pampering Liam, packing him off to the local shops armed with a hastily scrawled shopping list and chastising him if he failed in this simple task (as he invariably did), were receding into distant memory. Part of her wished that things could be back as they were, just a few years previously, when she had shared the house, fairly noisily, with all three sons.

On the other hand, part of her felt wildly excited. Like Liam, she felt betwixt two worlds although resolutely, more and more, she had refused to allow this new found fame to lift her beyond the comforts of her social setting. Pressure from the well-meaning lads, attempting to buy her "a mansion in Ireland", had been fiercely resisted.

"Why should I want to move?" she asked the *Manchester Evening News'* homely Rosemary Barratt, one of the few reporters she had allowed through her front door. "My life and my friends are here in Burnage. I get people in the street saying, 'When are you going? The boys are millionaires' and I think there must be something wrong with me. They might be millionaires and, if they are, they certainly aren't going to pile the lot on me. I'm quite happy and I don't need to ask them for things. I'm not into big houses, I'm quite happy with a roof over my head. I wouldn't say to them, 'Now it's your turn to look after me' because that's not the way I am."

This statement, although hardly untypical since similar paragraphs can be found lurking in a hundred rock star biogs, did, nevertheless, ring true. Peggy was often seen, out and about, enjoying the cosy anti-glamour of Burnage, flitting into the local cafés, excitedly flicking through pop magazines in the newsagents, crying softly while watching her boys perform on television. Each rock mag image, each performance on television, carried her back to simpler times – not so easy when your youngest son turns up, unannounced, on the doorstep, a beaming Patsy Kensit locked onto his arm.

"Why didn't you tell me you were coming, I'd have tidied up," she'd panic, naturally, but would, nevertheless, enjoy the glimpse into a different world. After all, it had only been a handful of years since Liam – very much the mother's boy of the three – would cling fiercely to her as they trundled around the local shops, or when Noel would return home from school and recite, in great detail, all the incidents of the day's lessons. Only later, when Noel's teacher rang and stated, "Noel's not been in school for weeks," would she realise the extent of the chicanery. However, whereas Noel would be thoughtful, often silent, generally conniving, Liam would always be loud, brash and arrogant.

"I remember going to Liam's Parents' Evening," she stated. "Apparently he was driving his teacher, Mrs Ward, around the twist. She said to me, 'Well, I don't know how on Earth you put up with him. I feel sorry for you because you have got him all the time and I have only got him for a few hours and, to be quite honest, at the end of the day, I have to go home and take a tablet.' And, to think this was when he was still at primary school."

* * *

Barely a mile away, in a gloomy three bedroom semi-detached, lives the estranged father, Thomas Gallagher. Having lost contact with the family over twelve years ago, Thomas, a country and western DJ, building site labourer and ex-pub singer, had watched the rise of his sons from a frustratingly long distance. He kept tabs on their progress by maintaining a swelling book of press cuttings, enjoying their success but longing for contact.

There seems little chance of that. Like Peggy, Thomas was plagued by reporters, although he was surprisingly adept at hiding his secret from his workmates. Oasis would constantly invade his lunch time breaks in the Ancoats pub, but to open up fully would be to launch into a complicated and rather sad little story to every passer by, every lunch time. Mostly, he just kept quiet although, as time passed, this would become more and more difficult.

It is Thomas Gallagher's claim that he purchased Noel's first guitar, when the Oasis leader was just thirteen, and installed in his son enough desire, drive and love of music to persevere through the difficult early months of learning when painful split fingertips discourage all but the keenest of young guitarists. The boys, however, especially as their fame mounted, have never spoken publicly of any affection towards their father, not even during the days before a bitter feud split the family in half.

According to the boys, and to Peggy, their early years were spent under the shadow of a man who allegedly fell into heavy bouts of drinking and constantly refused to allow his wages to filter into, let alone fuel, the family budget. This penny pinching - though Thomas insists there are two sides to the story - came to a head one day in 1984, when Noel, then 17 and tired of constant feuding, rose to his mother's defence and engaged in a struggle with his father which became so violent that an ambulance had to be called.

The boys' final and lasting vision of their father was the sight of him trudging bloodily away to the ambulance. They have never spoken to him since. Peggy immediately moved the boys to a nearby council house.

The fatherless household did not become a picture of domestic bliss. In fact, famously, the boys would fall into an intense sibling rivalry with Liam, then only 11, breaking out of his shell to crave the constant attention of a natural performer while Noel, conversely, fell into comparative introversion, spending longer and longer alone with his guitar and a pile of Beatles songbooks. Even as a teen and pre-teen, Noel and Liam Gallagher were, unwittingly, cementing a perfect rock band partnership and, throughout their story, things fall together in an eerily perfect manner.

There can be little doubt that the furious sibling rivalry, the arguments and the arrogant venom that would spice their songs in later years, can be traced back to those early childhood experiences. It was clearly here, deep in a volatile household, that a spirit of punk was duly born.

Peggy: "I remember Liam coming home from school, he would be so hyped up he would start jibing and picking on Paul, and then he would start on Noel and Noel would only take so much before his eyebrows would droop and the fighting would start...not vicious, but often wild."

The oldest of the brothers, Paul, could, if he wished, claim more responsibility than his father for instructing Noel through his first few guitar chords. When Oasis were nudging the top of the US album charts, he was still living at home, claiming £45 a week dole after losing his job as a gas fitter, managing the local band Performance and attempting to make headway as a music industry contact for a number of up and coming bands. Paul's character contrasts sharply with the other two.

"Paul was an easy boy to bring up," says Peggy. "He always did what you told him. I don't remember him ever getting into any of the usual rigmaroles the others got into. He was the total opposite. At Parents' Evening, the teachers used to say, 'Your Paul is such a pleasure to teach.' Absolutely the opposite of Liam."

At one stage, Paul, Noel and Liam would all work as gas mains layers for the same company, a situation accepted by Noel and Paul as a way of swelling the household coffers but hugely disliked by Liam. "I wasn't put on this earth to be a gas fitter," he would exclaim. And neither, perhaps, was Paul, who believes and hopes that lightning may well strike again within the very same household.

"More than anything in the world," said Peggy in March 1996, "I want Paul's band, Performance, to be successful."

CHAPTER TWO
Cosmic Advisor!

The flight path from Heathrow to destinations in America skims above Ashton-Under-Lyne, a redundant mill town, replenished by redevelopment and etched darkly into the edge of the Pennines on the east side of Manchester. It was later calculated that at the precise moment when Noel Gallagher was running nervously through his vocal audition with Inspiral Carpets, the tragically famous 'bombed' aircraft crashed into a Lockerbie hillside. A report in a local weekly paper later that week suggested gloomily, and perhaps speculatively, that had it not been for certain delays at Heathrow, the bomb would have exploded directly above Ashton. Few people took comfort from that.

The events at the audition paled into insignificance as the world struggled to 'understand' the reason for the tragedy, or pinpoint the blame. Nevertheless, during the days that followed, Noel Gallagher would spend many hours wondering quite why his spirited attempt to prize his way into the recently depleted line up of Inspiral Carpets had apparently failed so miserably.

The audition took place, perhaps fittingly, in a cleverly assembled 'hotch potch' of a studio which nestled just inside the catacombed shell of a redundant textile mill. The studio was named The Mill, after a band that its owner, Clint Boon, had played in alongside Stone Roses bassist Manny.

Boon's feverish and unswerving devotion towards his music, and indeed his tireless sense of self promotion, had seen him manage the promising Oldham band T' Challa Grid, then kick-start the punkily psychedelic Inspiral Carpets. This band, heavily flavoured by Boon's distinctive swirling organ sound, so rare among the legions of sub-Smiths outfits who chundered away in the small time clubs and pubs of north Manchester, had initially surfaced via a spate of Manchester gigs where their fairly staid visuals would be complemented by a Boon orchestrated 'slide projection' screen. The idea, courageously simplistic as it was, was to create a kind of 'underground atmosphere', a psychedelic swirl not seen, at least in Manchester, since the early seventies progressive era had crumbled to a halt in the city's seedier rock venues.

Noel Gallagher had latched onto Inspiral Carpets at an early stage in their development, catching their spirited live sets at the tiny Boardwalk venue. They provided support for the embryonic Happy Mondays at the larger International and even at a ludicrous council-run open air multi-band event, which took place in Albert Square beneath the severe shadows of Manchester Town Hall.

"Noel just started to become a regular face," says Boon. "I don't know quite where we first began talking, but we would see him at gigs, more and more, he'd be hanging around, watching us dismantle the equipment, everything."

Gallagher had actually plucked up enough courage to talk to Boon when he caught the organist taping a Stone Roses gig. He requested that Boon send him a copy of the tape for that night he had fallen in love with the Roses, with the look, the sound and with the inspired and partially free form guitar work of John Squire. Gallagher soon found himself falling deeper and deeper into musical conversation with the affable Boon.

The conversations, which continued backstage at various venues, would see the pair mapping out their areas of influence, with Gallagher, happy to languish in the role of pupil, allowing Boon to talk endlessly, as he does, about all manner of music forms, from the American mid-Sixties punk of The Seeds, to the English R&B boom, to the glorious Manchester punk scene. Boon had been a regular at the legendary punk venue, The Electric Circus, home to his favourite band, The Fall, and beyond. Gallagher seemed content to allow this information to sink in. He enjoyed the way that Boon seemed capable of shading the background to the music forms he, himself had only recently discovered. His love of The Smiths, for example, was only deepened by Boon's verbal detailing.

Inspiral Carpets, however, had yet to evolve into a major force and, indeed, their initial burst onto the scene, via a smattering of gigs and two lively EP's on Playtime Records, had stuttered rather messily to a halt, following the departure of singer Steven Hull and bass player Dave Swift. Inspired by the rumour that the 'Inspies' were seeking another vocalist, Gallagher courageously offered his services, even producing his own demo tape – four songs slammed hastily onto the tape via a four track – which he hoped might be segued into the 'Carpets' repertoire.

Despite a growing awareness that his songs weren't exactly awful, he arrived at The Mill in a state of deep trepidation. The audition, during which Gallagher performed two Inspirals' songs, 'Joe' and 'Keep The Circle Around' and The Stones' 'Gimme Shelter', was traumatic, although it was softened by the sense of band camaraderie, into which he slipped with ease. Boon, however, knew straight away that the Gallagher method of singing, although not without power or a certain charm, was simply not the kind of thing the band had been looking for. "It was too punky for us...we were seeking some kind of Sinatra type thing at the time," says Boon. Mysteriously, the successful applicant, Tom Hingley, hardly fulfilled that criteria either.

Despite this rejection, and perhaps initially to ease Gallagher's obvious hurt, the band decided to offer him a job, part time initially but, given the success which swiftly arrived, rising to full time employment. Almost unwittingly, Noel Gallagher had become the roadie/secretary/merchandiser and, in Boon's words, 'cosmic adviser'. Without ever playing or singing a note for them, Gallagher became part of Inspiral Carpets. It was a liaison that was to last for over three years.

*   *   *

Within weeks, with Hingley taking over the vocal spot and with Gallagher leaning closer and closer to the band's inner politics, The Inspirals wrenched themselves away from Playtime and launched themselves into a remarkable period of recording, releasing and self-merchandising, carving themselves a lucrative niche in the burgeoning 'Madchester' explosion, fronted by the twin wonders of Stone Roses and Happy Mondays.

The Carpets may not have quite reached the heights scaled by those two – although at their peak, and at the peak of 'Madchester', they did manage to sell out the 11,000 capacity G-Mex venue in Manchester, and draw considerable crowds in America, Europe and Japan. Inspiral Carpets soon became famous for their industrious professionalism – a quality which was certainly lacking in both the hedonistic Mondays and appallingly slothful Roses – and Gallagher was happy to immerse himself in their affairs. He was happy to play the role of 'cog' in the Carpets' machinery, organising the fan club mail-outs, distributing the famous Inspiral Carpets Moo – Cool As Fuck T-Shirts and edging his way closer and closer to the heart of the band's internal politics. He was alert, bright as a button, and ever willing to learn anything and everything about the music business. To the band, he seemed a Godsend, for such enthusiasm is a rare commodity amongst the 'loyal' periphery of a hard working band.

Gallagher was more than a mere office boy. Even as a roadie, much to the band's delight, his talents proved universal. He began, meekly, as Boon's roadie, taking care of the keyboards, although it soon became clear that he was equally, if not more capable of attending to the drums and, most specifically, the guitars. That Gallagher could play all the instruments initially surprised the band who were equally impressed with his ability to learn quickly, and grasp more than the mere rudiments of the PA set up. Gallagher was intelligently soaking up every aspect of the music business. In a sense, the ferocious work rate and DIY aspect of The Carpets suited him as pupil and, for a good two years, they regarded him as indispensable.

On a personal level, Gallagher ingratiated himself fully with the band, in particular Boon, with whom he would often share a hotel room. There was an honesty about his enthusiasm, too, for although he would become involved with every single business transaction, every aspect of the gigging and merchandising, he never made any secret of the fact that he had no intention of remaining a roadie for long. He longed to better himself and found the Carpets equally willing to share their artistic problems with him. No song writing session would be complete without Gallagher's input, and soon his rather frank appraisals or dismissals – "It's fookin' shite Clint" or, "That's a real gem, good 'n lads" – were taken very seriously indeed by the band. This precocious drive would land him in many song writing discussions, mostly with Boon, who duly noted an increasing sophistication in his attitude.

"I knew he was writing songs...that became more and more apparent and perhaps we should have taken a bit more notice, but, to be honest, we were just busy all the time," admits Boon, who couldn't possibly have known that his personal roadie and good mate would one day attain superstar status.

As the nineties wore on, and as Madchester began to recede, and indeed become ingloriously unfashionable, the Carpets found themselves, despite a solid block of minor hit singles, having to work harder and harder to maintain their high profile. It was during an intense period of work, in 1992, that things began to sour a little.

Boon: "Well, things began to change. It is no secret that he (Noel) likes the drugs and it was the drug thing that made him something different. He became unemployable to some extent. That was one of the reasons we had to let him go. It was one of the saddest things for us. I mean, we had sacked all kinds of people, accountants, managers, tour managers but sacking Noel was the only time things really hurt. But by that time, we knew that, at least, he had got something going with Oasis. It was the end of 1993, we had just returned from a five week tour of Europe. It was a hard tour and we were all under a lot of pressure...and the 'white dust' doesn't help. Drugs were 30% of the reason why he went."

But only 30%! In truth, the Inspiral Carpets 'empire' had lessened considerably by this time. Back in Manchester, in their base at the media, music and creative industries site at 24, New Mount Street (another converted mill) the workload had subsided to a slow trickle. Gallagher found himself sitting in the office, staring glassily at the walls, mailing out the odd T-shirt, answering three phone calls a day instead of fifty and generally dreaming about his own, lowly rock career. As far as The Inspirals were concerned, ridding themselves of Gallagher was the best move for both parties, and so it turned out, though Gallagher was still considerably stunned by the news.

"Yeah, Noel was gutted," says Boon. "I mean, he had lost a great job, travelling around the world, having a great time really. It could have been awful for him but we sensed that his mind was elsewhere. Maybe we didn't guess that Oasis, who had started by then, would be so big, but we had an inkling that something would happen. None of us were surprised."

Noel's work with Inspiral Carpets, whether he was suffering from chemical over-indulgence or not, certainly suffered. His enthusiasm of yore began to wane. The rot had set in, back in 1991 when, on telephoning his mother from America, Noel was stunned to learn that younger brother Liam had joined a band. It was a shock, to say the least, although Noel's expectations of the outfit were understandably low. Indeed, Liam had never shown the slightest inkling towards music, until, that is, the day that Noel had taken him to a Stone Roses gig in Manchester. Ever since that day - May 28, 1988, Noel's 21st birthday – Liam had secretly nurtured dreams of pop stardom.

Staring at Stone Roses singer Ian Brown that day, Liam became famously addicted to the delicious arrogance that can be adopted and enjoyed by a rock band in ascendancy. Brown, of course, was often an absurdly blasé performer, sauntering about the stage – hardly moving at all – as if engrossed in the music while often making absolutely no concessions whatsoever to the notion of 'entertainment'.

Liam thought this 'stance', this 'attitude', was wholly intoxicating and, naturally, like the crowd who swirled around him that day at the Anti Clause 28 gig, he carried a little of the arrogance home with him and he would never lose it. There was nothing at all new about this, indeed, the attitude has been passed down the generations. It is often stronger, more intoxicating, in the early stages of a band, as anyone who saw the early Who, the Sex Pistols or indeed, The Fall or PiL would certainly testify.

If Liam Gallagher was ever to front a band, he promised himself, he'd be exactly the same as Brown. He wouldn't give a shit. He'd be there for himself, fully, and people could either feed off that and become similarly inspired or they could simply please themselves and ignore it. Until that Roses gig, Liam had actually been wholly dismissive of Noel's constant enthusing over music and all his bedroom guitar strumming.

"It used to really fuckin' annoy me," said Liam, "sharing a room with someone forever messin' about with a fucking guitar. I'd say, 'Shut up with that bunch of crap you are playing, you can't play it anyway', I was more into football and just being a little scally and all that."

Music surged into Liam's life following that Roses gig. Legend has it, though nobody seems to want to substantiate it, that Liam immediately purchased four copies of the Stone Roses' classic début album following the gig. He might well have done, for his infatuation with the band verged on the obsessive.

"I couldn't get 'I Wanna Be Adored' out of me head for years," he later said, "I just lived with it, going round and round."

CHAPTER THREE
Backbeat...The Word On The Street

Despite Liam's growing musical awareness, it still shocked Noel to think of his younger brother singing in a band before he'd actually made the same transition from punter to performer. The band, named The Rain, was little more than a competent and typically Mancunian low brow unit, brimming with stifled Smiths and Joy Division references, pumping out the kind of music that would seep, so wearily, from a thousand rehearsal rooms in the north west of England. It was solid, deadening rock, devoid of light and genuine inspiration.

The Rain's original singer had quit, leaving three members, guitarist Paul 'Bonehead' Arthurs, bass guitarist Paul 'Guigs' McGuigan and drummer Tony McCarroll to stagger along, occasionally sending four track demo recordings to the *Manchester Evening News*, hurrying to the newsagents on a Friday afternoon to see if they had scored the merest mention. Local Burnage lads, they had known the Gallaghers for at least ten years, although the subject of music had never previously been raised. On arriving home, Noel, acting very much the part of the world-weary rock biz know-all, rather condescendingly went to see the band in action at Manchester's Boardwalk on August 18, 1991.

They were sandwiched between aspiring locals The Catchmen and Sweet Jesus. By this point the name had changed to Oasis, though it will forever remain in doubt if any of them realised quite how multi-faceted this new name would be. The choice of name would, in time, become shrouded in mystery, made all the more enigmatic by Noel Gallagher's constant stream of disinformation regarding the moniker and

Liam's insistence that "...it never meant anything."

At various times, the band have declared, "It was just a poster on a wall...it was a tax office....it was a really cool local sportswear shop...it was taken from The Swindon Oasis, a venue where The Carpets played....it was a local 'take away'...it was the name of an aquarium where ex-Inspirals manager Anthony Boggiano once bought a load of fish..."

It matters not, of course, where the original inspiration came from, and one senses that the band would warm to such connotations as, "an oasis in a sea of mediocrity". Oasis, the name, carries with it other localised meanings.

Throughout the seventies, a brash, young and rather violent myriad of teen fashion clothes shops could be found gathered famously together at the top of the stairs, above Manchester's notorious Underground Market. The complex was rife with latter day skinhead muggings and football violence; indeed, even the purchase of a pair of 'parallels' would be followed by a traditional 'chicken run', through an ambuscade of hateful stares and arms that would lunge at your new acquisition. The complex was called The Oasis Centre, the name itself a throwback to an infamous Manchester R&B club in the sixties, which always used to pride itself in the phrase 'the north's top teenage rendezvous.'

Noel Gallagher's initial impression was, to say the least, muted. Backstage at The Boardwalk, he complimented the band on their musicianship, but openly declared, "I think you're shit, really, to tell you the truth, because you haven't got any songs." This stark, honest declaration, which would have immediately pushed most bands onto the defensive, was greeted with enthusiasm from the lads who frankly agreed. Noel ran through a song he'd written when he had worked for British Gas. The song was called 'Live Forever' and the band, far from displaying musicianly envy, seemed massively impressed. The simple solution, they suggested, would be if Noel would write them some more like that.

It was an early pivotal moment with Noel Gallagher immediately seizing the initiative. Retiring to his Burnage bedroom, he duly wrote a couple of precocious songs, still intending them only to provide some kind of artistic impetus for his brother's band. The band, however, had other ideas and, sensing that Noel Gallagher was the missing link, they pleaded with him to join.

Noel Gallagher's terms were hard. He knew, full well, that he had spent the past five years planning this moment and no amount of musical lazyitus or ineptitude was going to see his chance wilt away. Still only half convinced that Oasis were the band he had been waiting for – after all, they were the first he'd bumped into so it was unlikely – he laid down the essential ground rules.

"Right," he declared, strongly in Boardwalk Rehearsal Room No.4, "If I join this band, and I mean it, right, you fucking belong to me seven days a week and we rehearse six nights a week and we are going for it big time." The band immediately agreed although, in retrospect, it seemed a ludicrous blag on Gallagher's behalf. After all, his song writing was completely untried and untested, even at basic local band level. None of the songs had ever been performed live and only a few scruffy demos had been produced during a five year period. All he was, in truth, was an ingloriously sacked roadie. Still, he seemed to have some kind of power, if not presence, and Liam seemed genuinely excited about the prospect of singing his brother's songs. That, in itself, was unusual.

Within weeks, the band found themselves surging through 'Live Forever', 'Rock And Roll Star' and 'Up In The Sky'. Despite a 'tightness' in the music, a fragile camaraderie began to build although the band members, including Liam, soon tired of Noel's bolstering arrogance. In his head, they duly noted, he was a pop star but nobody was listening, nobody was turning up at the gigs and, more importantly, nobody seemed in the remotest bit impressed with anything they were producing. On numerous occasions, the bonding of Oasis crumbled to muffled, grumpy meetings in the local pubs.

Outside the rehearsal room doors, the boom of Madchester was receding and, inevitably, a short cold snap of unhipness was settling on the city. There were even reports that Oasis were Stone Roses copyists, and the brothers' stark, dark leers hardly dispelled this rumour. They made demo tapes like any band but, mostly, refused to allow them to circulate around the usual motley collection of local venue owners, journalists and DJ's. To all intents and purposes, and much to the annoyance of all band members other than Noel Gallagher, Oasis were superstars only within the confines of their rehearsal rooms.

"I remember being approached by them," says Darren Poyzer, booker for Ashton-Under-Lyne's lively Witchwood venue, "but I refused them a gig. I wouldn't even put them on the bottom of a local band bill because they refused to send me a demo and displayed an attitude that seemed rather insulting. There were a good many excellent local bands around at the time who I felt were far more deserving."

Nevertheless, a set, of sorts, was coming together amid the downbeat musicianly bonhomie and furious gossip of The Boardwalk rehearsal rooms, an ex-Victorian school, initially containing a tiny theatre, the rehearsal rooms and upstairs venue. It had, literally, evolved slowly from a crumbly, cramped shell into a natural catalyst for the Manchester scene since the mid-eighties and it was soon rife with talk about Gallagher's band. Initially dismissed as dullards with naïve, overblown notions of their own worth, talk of the band's tightness and confidence soon rippled through the Boardwalk and the musician-filled pubs which pepper the Knott Mill area.

They made a clumsy début on the Boardwalk stage on October 19, 1991, when they blasted their way somewhat ineptly through four songs in front of 12 people and Boardwalk manager Colin Sinclair. Unknown to Sinclair, and as a somewhat self- defeating, not to say infantile prank, the band had put up a £40 entrance fee sign.

Occasionally after that Oasis would venture upstairs to surge through spirited support sets to fringe bands such as the ever optimistic and poppy Milltown Brothers and a circle of post-Madchester hopefuls who would push for coverage in the *Manchester Evening News*. Likewise, Oasis passed a demo tape to the *Evening News'* pop writer Terry Christian, whose column, instigated years before the television programme, was also called The Word. Christian knew Noel Gallagher from his days with the Inspirals, when the former would burrow a lonely indie furrow into the usually more maintstream playlists at Piccadilly Radio.

"I knew Noel and was scared to listen to his tape in case it was shit," states Christian, "and, to be honest, I can't say it sounded that special, though Noel would later play me the songs in person, and they sounded great." Christian's mate, Craig Cash, a night time 'indie' DJ on Stockport's KFM Radio (which began life as a proud pirate, later to be swamped by the bland and useless Signal Radio) picked up on the tape and played it nightly to his small huddle of listeners, some of whom, it must be noted, were scattered about the Bohemian bedsits of nearby Didsbury.

That stated, Oasis were very much adrift in a local band ocean and, in post-Madchester Manchester, this ocean was dispiritingly vast. There were twenty or thirty bands of promise who never managed to make the slightest impact. It didn't seem that Oasis would be any different. It is with pride, therefore, that the man who would inherit Christian's *Manchester Evening News* pop column, Chris Sharratt, then pop editor of *City Life* magazine, would review the tape for the Christmas double issue. Sharratt, undoubtedly the first journalist to feign interest in the band, wrote "Oasis go for the dramatic build up here, first acoustic guitar, then pattering drums and bass, then vocals. A bit nasally in places, sort of like a demo from Northside but with a cold. In fact, the whole song is in that Northside vein. The second track's more urgent and weird, sort of Inspiral's on psychedelics...interesting, but I'm not too excited."

Although in essence Oasis were a mere handful of low key gigs old and Liam, in particular, was still very much a beginner, Noel Gallagher felt justifiably frustrated about the band being adrift in the class of 1992. He would later describe his peers as, "a load of crap losers...I always knew we were far too good to remain among that lot."

*   *   *

By May 1992, The Oasis repertoire had swelled into an admirable 45 minute live set and, indeed, had already begun to fluctuate and change, as Noel Gallagher's song writing pace began to quicken. The set's centrepiece would be 'Columbia', which would eventually survive although 'Better Let You Know', 'Acoustic', 'Take Me', 'Must Be The Music', 'Snakebite', 'See The Sun' and 'Colour My Life' would ultimately fall by the wayside. The latter three songs surfaced on a hasty four track demo that circulated, mainly unheard, around Manchester.

There was an unholy scramble in Manchester during the summer of 1992 when television journalist and Factory Records boss Anthony H. Wilson, his partner Yvette Livesey and Simply Red manager Elliot Rashman instigated the first 'In The City' music seminar, a three day orgy of inebriated 'biz talk' and sycophantic bleating, complimented by a splattering of gigs in the city centre. With the entire pack of British A & R men and tea boy talent scouts in town, every small band in Manchester would constantly bug seminar co-ordinator Bindi Binning for a chance to play. To the band's huge delight, and to the disgust of practically all who rehearsed around them, Oasis scored a lowly support spot in the decrepit Venue, a cellar bar just thirty yards along Whitworth Street from The Hacienda. A mass of A & R men did actually turn up for the gig, though all of them were there to see the main band, Skywalker.

Though Oasis by all accounts performed a spirited set, not one record company person even bothered to make small talk with them. This wasn't particularly surprising, for the music industry operates on a sheep-like mentality in regard to talent scouting. Until a pack of A & R men begin to chase a band, and thus instigate a bargaining frenzy, there is little point in showing serious, or even passing interest. That night, the industry had flocked, albeit half-heartedly, to see Skywalker. The fact that the support band, although undeniably a bit ragged at the time, would one day revitalise the British music industry on a global scale, and practically single-handedly at that, makes the occasion, in retrospect, seem all the more absurd, all the more typical.

As it happens, the band were fired up for the gig. On the

previous night they had trouped down to the BBC's New Broadcasting House to perform a live session for Radio 5's innovative *Hit The North* programme, normally hosted by Mark Radcliffe with help and interjections from producer and comic sidekick, Marc Riley. Mainman Radcliffe, however, was away on holiday that night, so New Order's evergreen socialite bass player, Peter Hook, stepped in, more for a laugh than anything else.

Hook was rather taken aback when confronted by a local band who truly didn't hold him in any kind of esteem. On the contrary, they were downright dismissive of his fairly forgivable affectations. "Your leather trousers are fucking awful, you affected tosser!" screamed Liam at one point.

Sneeringly, Hook told the young upstart that he would never get into the Hacienda again.

"Who wants to go down that fookin' shithole, anyway," scoffed Liam.

Hook wasn't amused, although Riley, noting that any other local band would be nothing less than awe-struck in the presence of a member of New Order, made a telling comment:

"If you could bottle that attitude, you could make a million."

CHAPTER FOUR
Me And Alan McGee

Noel Gallagher, frustrated and ultra keen to lift his group out of the 'local band' shadows once and for all, installed a new, granite-hard regime for Oasis to follow. Boardwalk rehearsals, which had slipped a little, were upped from twice a week to five times a week, much to the chagrin of those bands who gathered around, at one point pinning a "find some riffs of your own" notice on the Oasis door.

One musician, a guitarist in a not-too-bad Factory outfit – who prefers to remain nameless, for obvious reasons – says: "We all hated Oasis in The Boardwalk, not because of their personalities, although they could be a really nasty bunch, but because they were constantly going over the same tried and tested riffs, over and over again. I suppose they should now be applauded for their commitment, but we were Manchester bands. And Manchester bands, traditionally, were always, always innovative."

"That was always the big thing. If a band could discover a new angle, like Joy Division, New Order, The Smiths, Happy Mondays, Stone Roses...all those bands, then they would be truly Mancs! It is a city of innovation. So it really annoyed us to see this bunch having no innovative notions at all. At one point they just kept playing a fucking T-Rex tune over and over. I think it became 'Cigarettes And Alcohol' in the end, but we couldn't see it, none of The Boardwalk bands. We all thought we were so cool, so ahead of the game, and yet this lot, so unlikely really, just walked right past the lot of us. It was unbelievable. Never in a million years would I have expected Oasis to get anywhere. Sometimes I still can't believe it. The last band in Manchester who you'd expect to get anywhere are now courted as the new Beatles...it's a funny old world."

Following the 'In The City' débacle, Noel Gallagher decided to push the band into some serious recording. He had just sent a barrage of tapes out to the record companies – a pointless exercise, really – including Creation, and had sat by his mum's telephone, waiting for the calls which, naturally, failed to materialise. Incensed by this lack of reaction, he contacted an old friend from the Inspirals days, Tony Griffiths from Liverpool's The Real People, who owned their own eight track recording studio. The scousers, in refreshing contrast to the back-biting competitiveness that existed in The Boardwalk, practically invited the band into the studio, pointing out the finer details of studio technique, in which Oasis were woefully inept, along the way.

Liverpool bands tend to look after each other and always have done, a state of affairs that stretches back to the days when the pleasing bonhomie of Liverpool's Bunnymen/ Teardrops crowd clashed sharply with Manchester's furiously competitive Joy Division/Fall/Buzzcocks circle in the late seventies.

Noel Gallagher's song writing improved immensely during the band's short exposure to scouse friendship. For Oasis, a bunch of insular stalwart Manchester City fans, this was something of a revelation. (That said, and for obvious reasons, most Man City fans retain a curious fondness for Liverpool). During this spell The Real People, and Tony Griffiths in particular, spent hours talking to Noel about the dynamics and construction of songs. Eventually this liaison would produce a nine song Oasis demo, a body of work that would evolve into their début album, *Definitely Maybe*.

The band's final appearance on the modest, though esteemed Boardwalk stage, would be on November 22, 1992, when they languished third on the bill below The Cherries and the highly rated Playtime Records band, Molly Half Head. The gig proved woefully portentous, for it ended in acrimony after Oasis had fallen into confrontation with The Cherries.

The Oasis set, rather surprisingly considering the short gigs they had played in the past, began to overrun, and The Cherries, not wishing to appear at the death of the evening, duly pulled the plug. Incensed, Liam chased around the club for the rest of the evening, attempting to locate, and punish, the culprits.

* * *

The swift transition of Oasis from this insular and lowly base to the position of the young darlings of Creation Records seems now to have been quite unrealistically smooth. It is perhaps important to point out that with Oasis, perhaps more than any other band, their astonishing and apparently effortless career path hides a postulating reality of in-fights, violent bickering and savage sibling rivalry.

Nevertheless, the volatile nature of the unit tended also to cement a hidden bond. In the inner world of Oasis, anything worth bothering about is worth scrapping about, and nothing, absolutely nothing, is ever allowed to fester. This might seem rather obvious, especially as the band's temperament and collective arrogance is now common knowledge, but such a bond is extremely rare. Few bands manage to solve their niggles with such positive energy.

It might also be noted that, despite The Rain's lack of a song writing spark, and possibly even because of it, they had developed a noticeably tight rhythm section, a perfect base to wrap around Noel Gallagher's songs. Whether the lads know, or will ever know, just how unlikely such a combination is, especially at the first attempt, is a matter of some doubt.

"I always knew we were brilliant," stated Noel on many occasions. Although the statement was undeniably true, it must be noted that every band, in every rehearsal bunker in England, also know just how brilliant they are, until events or lack of real talent or incompatibility tends to prove otherwise. There are occasions, though, when things slot into place so effortlessly that one tends to sit back in wonder at the sheer power of the hand of fate.

To be encamped amid a slew of bottom rung local bands is a position that swamps ninety five percent of hopefuls, and frequently signals the premature end of their careers.

Nevertheless, when talent and sheer unadulterated confidence combine...who knows?

*   *   *

In May of 1993 Oasis, desperate to play somewhere outside of Manchester, accepted an untempting offer from one of the bands with whom they shared rehearsal rooms, the all girl Sister Lovers. Sister Lovers had been offered a support slot in Glasgow to burgeoning Creation Records band 18 Wheeler at the hardly prestigious King Tut's Wah Wah Hut and, rather presumptuously, they informed Oasis they could get them a spot on the bottom of the bill.

Inspired by the thought of Glasgow adventure, they took with them their sorry tangle of equipment and an unholy huddle of half-inebriated mates, all crammed purposefully into the back of the proverbial Transit van. This scenario, especially in the early days of a band, generally leads to either disaster or disillusionment for the arrival at such a venue is, more often than not, wrapped in anti-climax. This date, it seemed, would be little different.

Subjected to a barrage of small minded, "Who are you? Oh no, you can't play here lads, the bill is full," talk from 'the management', Oasis and their menacing gaggle of mates regrouped in the corner, swiftly worked out a game plan that had always stood them in good stead on the terraces at Maine Road, and promptly instructed 'the management' that, should they not be allowed to perform, a riot would almost certainly ensue.

Perhaps the most astonishing chapter in the Oasis story was about to unfold, for from this comedic, Bad News scenario, Oasis stumbled immediately past the ludicrous A & R talent scouting system. Noel Gallagher, forever glancing back to that night, has often muttered about the band being "fated" to perform before the wise eyes of Creation boss Alan McGee, and the events of the evening certainly add weight to that theory.

McGee, now some way beyond the tiresome task of hanging

around seedy venues for hour after hour watching band after band, was accustomed to waltzing into a club five minutes before or after his band appeared on stage. Due to a misunderstanding however, and the fact that he was accompanied by his sister who, McGee later stated, "doesn't own a watch", he arrived at the venue very early, only to discover that 18 Wheeler were not due to appear for another two hours.

Settling into the rear of the deserted club, his attention was arrested by an unsightly gaggle of bolshy Mancunians, physically and verbally forcing their way towards the stage. Enjoying this unexpected cabaret, and sucking on a bottle of Jack Daniels, McGee witnessed, along with exactly eighteen other people, a four song set which climaxed with a frantic version of 'I Am The Walrus'.

McGee was unusually ecstatic, immediately informing the startled Liam Gallagher that he was the perfect blend of John Lennon and John Lydon. With comic urgency, the Creation boss leapt into the dressing room, and began shouting, bewildering the half-intoxicated band. "Five album deal," he yelled. "Cheque book, here...now...has ye got a record deal...d'youse want one?"

At one point Liam thought that McGee had been planted by the promoter to act out some kind of joke.

"We thought he was taking the piss, because he was all Armani'd up and was a bit of a smoothie," Liam said later, adding, "and he has stated to me later that he didn't even know what the fuck he signed the band for. I think something must just have got him in the heart...he sensed something...odd really, 'cos we were pretty crap, that night."

This bizarre meeting, as if plucked from a corny, parodic rock 'n' roll novel, seems certain to be set firmly into rock mythology and, even now, is difficult to believe. After chatting to McGee about all manner of things, from guitars to cars to football, the band staggered from the club, swimming in the outrageous knowledge that they had, in effect, just signed to Creation. Although at least 20 other offers would flood in, including an offer to "double whatever Creation are offering" from the U2 owned Mother Records (this tempted Noel, not the money, but the association with U2 who, despite their proverbial 'unhipness', would always be cited as a major influence), it was Creation who would stay the course.

CHAPTER FIVE
A Reactionary Chic

Sometimes things are just meant to be. Before Alan McGee arrived in their lives, Oasis were less than happy about allowing their demo tapes to circulate around places where their ideas might be seized upon, not that anything dangerously innovatory might be found lurking in Gallagher's song writing.

A natural reactionary, he enjoyed though mistrusted the simplistic beats of the then dominant dance scene, stubbornly preferring to slice mighty chunks from his favourite, and trusted writers. In an age when the 'song', as such, had taken something of a back seat, and even the Stone Roses seemed to be levelling into a funk jam, Noel Gallagher took great delight in borrowing from the Kinks, from T Rex, the Stooges, Neil Young and more. Surprisingly, it wasn't until later that Gallagher swayed mildly towards psychedelia, especially as his former employers, Inspiral Carpets, had borrowed so heavily from the psychedelic garage bands of the American west coast, in particular Sky Saxon And The Seeds. There was one other band, of course, whose dominance over the Manchester scene up until, and beyond, their demise in 1987, could never be questioned: The Smiths.

Naturally, Noel Gallagher had leaned heavily towards the Johnny Marr side of the Smiths conundrum, ever since catching the band as a teenager. By chance, Gallagher knew Marr's actor brother, Ian – from nights in The Hacienda – and, for once, he decided to hand over a demo tape, instructing Ian to pass it on to his brother. This wasn't a particularly unusual occurrence, for Ian Marr was forever passing tapes across and Johnny, always one to keep his feet firmly on Manchester ground, spent more time than most listening to the often woefully uninspired local band demo's.

Rarely, if ever, did Marr find it necessary to respond to these entreaties, but not a flicker of hesitation creased his features as he reached for the telephone and dialled the number scribbled across the Oasis demo. Noel Gallagher seemed somewhat phased as Marr told him that his tape was amazing. Gallagher's reply was filled with large gaps – he rushed into the kitchen at one point in order to let out a rather unbecoming howl of delight – and, hardly believing his luck, agreed to accompany Marr for a drink in a city centre bar the very next day.

The pair fell into heady and largely impenetrable guitar-speak revolving around Neil Young, the Sex Pistols and The Beatles. Asked what guitar he used, Gallagher proudly replied, "I've got this 1970 Epiphone Riviera, tobacco brown, that I bought in a shop in Doncaster." This was, apparently, a perfect reply, for Marr was an aficionado of the vintage guitar shops of England. To Gallagher's surprise, Marr exclaimed, "Fucking hell, do you want to go up there tomorrow?" Silly question. The next day the pair drove to Doncaster, with Gallagher hanging onto Marr's every word, watching in awe as the former Smith began spending absurd amounts of money.

Still 'dole queued' and feverishly hungry for success, Gallagher, if he didn't know before, knew now exactly what he wanted to be. He wanted to be Johnny Marr...and then some.

Marr's involvement would prove vital. After catching the band live at Manchester's Hop And Grapes, and learning about the grasping hand of Creation, he informed the manager of his band, Electronic – Marcus Russell, from Ignition Management – about "this fucking amazing band from Burnage." Russell was a cultured, undemonstrative music industry professional who had guided Marr expertly since the messy implosion of The Smiths and who didn't encroach too heavily on the artist's work. He was the perfect choice.

Russell's first experience of Oasis was watching them support Dodgy, and he came to the immediate conclusion that this was just the kind of gig they would be unwise to pursue. Nevertheless he agreed to take them on. And so, with little thought, absolutely no master plan whatsoever, and certainly no Machiavellian dabblings, Noel Gallagher had walked directly into his perfect band, formed an alliance with, in his words, "the best record company in the world," and fallen into the welcoming arms of one of the few rock managers capable of fully understanding, promoting and catapulting the band into the spotlight of a world stage. No wonder he retains a fatalistic view of life.

Signing to Creation proved painless and most signed acts, noting the speed with which Oasis were ushered onto the roster, could be forgiven for thinking that the extraordinary meeting with Creation was something of a hype - only it wasn't. Pen met paper on October 2, 1993, and the only hiccup was Noel Gallagher's objection to photographs of The Farm that adorned the Creation walls. This was a reasonably natural objection, for The Farm, Liverpudlian scallies to a man, had in the past often clashed rather messily with Manchester acts.

"It's no joke," insisted Noel, "I'm not signing anything until those posters go."

The truth is that Oasis were a perfect Creation band, a fact disputed by few, although Manchester's Factory Records were alerted to the cause after their A & R man Phil Saxe – who had brought Happy Mondays to the label and who possesses two of the finest ears in Manchester – had chanced upon an Oasis demo tape. Although Factory's hometown ethic might well have perfectly suited Oasis, the label was sagging from a rather cumbersome post-Madchester roster, and simply had no room and a shrinking wallet. Rather ironically, Saxe also turned up at a Factory meeting at the same time, waving a universally ignored demo tape by Pulp.

"I knew Oasis and Pulp were going to be major forces in the near future, but I couldn't do anything about either of them," said Factory boss, Tony Wilson.

Noel Gallagher's recollection of the Factory 'near miss' is rather different. Talking to Radio 1, Gallagher stated, "He (Wilson) went into a big speech about how the music business was all overrun by cockneys and how 'baggy' (the Stone Roses, Happy Mondays-led Madchester scene) had been killed by them. We just thought, 'Alright, Tone...up the workers.' Two weeks later he rang us up and said the tape was 'too baggy'!"

But Creation suited them more than the often rather insular Factory. They would spend evenings at Alan McGee's flat, endlessly listening to Big Star and pretending to like them. More and more, McGee realised that his feverish and somewhat embarrassing actions that night at King Tut's were justified. There were strained moments, especially when Noel Gallagher strongly objected, and only partially in jest, to sharing a roster with artists like Slowdive, Swervedriver and Shonen Knife who, according to the Gallagher school of informed rock critique, were "absolutely the biggest pile of shite I have ever heard in me life." On a trip to Creation's London office, the band were given licence to dip into the Creation warehouse, though, with the exception of a couple of cassettes, none of the band could find anything they wished to own. Nevertheless they soon warmed fully to McGee and his often unbridled enthusiasm.

Noel Gallagher's song writing improved week by week as he revitalised fading influences and filtered them into his songs. Lyrically, however, things seemed to be twisting rather more absurdly. Not a natural lyric writer, there was a certain emptiness languishing in his songs which would remain there to become something of an Oasis trademark. The lyric lines slotted neatly into place, more like guitar riffs than emotive expressions, and they relied heavily on the listener's interpretation. Ironically, this unpretentious, honest and simplistic approach would serve the band well, setting them apart from the hundreds of post-Morrisseys or sub-Bowies. That stated, the lack of pure emotive lyric writing would remain a gaping flaw in a band who always regarded themselves to be nothing less than the best.

In truth, lyrical inspiration could come from literally anywhere. On December 19, 1993, the band were in Liverpool's Pink Museum studios, desperately searching for lyrical inspiration. It duly arrived in the form of a Rottweiler by the name of Elsa, who belonged to sound engineer Dave Scott. Poor Elsa, not at all welcome in the studio, suffered terribly from wind. "She must have eaten an entire packet of Alka Seltzer," someone noted. Hence the conception of the famous but meaningless line from 'Supersonic' which simply made reference to that very same dog.

As far as McGee was concerned, he had the most important band in the world on his books. An initial Creation-funded demo tape, which included raw versions of 'Bring It On Down', 'Married With Children', 'Digsy's Dinner', 'Alive' and 'Do Yer Wanna Be A Spaceman?', confirmed his excitement, and soon McGee would be telephoning the Gallagher's, often in the early hours of the morning, enthusing solidly about his belief in their immense potential.

McGee also encouraged and nurtured Liam Gallagher's rather nervous, Rottenesque whine. "Jeez, maan," he screamed at Liam after hearing the singer stretch a few syllables across whole spans of song, "you gotta go for that, you gotta do that in the recording, it's Johnny Rotten, maan, jeeez, the potential...the potential!"

But 'potential', it remained. Perhaps unwisely, the band continued to perform live, supporting all manner of local acts, but they soon realised that signing a Creation recording contract didn't necessarily guarantee kudos on the small gig circuit. Indeed, it tended to inspire envy which fuelled unpleasant back-biting. Equally, the paying public remained unimpressed. In Leeds, where this writer witnessed the band's storming set falling maniacally into the kind of feedback climax that would have made Iggy And The Stooges proud, they were greeted by the kind of applause normally reserved for a nil-nil draw in the Beezer Homes League. After slamming to a halt, the band uttered a fantastic, sarcastic, "Thank you!", before sneering their way, ever so slowly, off the stage. But audience indifference can strengthen a band's resolve.

Strangely enough, following some aghast press reports which surfaced in the wake of the band's swift signing, there was a mini backlash before the band had even released a record. Creation rather cleverly decided to 'shunt out' a white label promotional 12" of 'Columbia', and push it shyly towards press and industry luminaries. This 'biz' release, although in raw mix form, was the result of some loose studio work, but it still managed to get play-listed by Radio 1, who took the unprecedented step of playing an unreleased single. This was confusing, as it seemed to feed the sycophantic clique-ishness that lies at the heart of the industry, the rock biz snootiness towards which Noel Gallagher had always professed a near-violent loathing.

"I want to write music for the guy who walks down the street to buy his copy of the Daily fooking Mirror and his 20 Bensons every day and he's got fuck all going for him," he would say, "...even if someone can't afford to buy our record, if they put on the radio while they are cleaning the 'ouse and whistle along and go 'fucking hell, did you 'ear that tune?' That's what it is all about."

*   *   *

At the start of 1994, flushed with the songs that seemed to be spilling from Noel Gallagher's head (although, by his own proud admission, they were mostly pieced together from his extensive and expanding knowledge of rock history), and fired by a sense of urgency, Oasis bounced like a pinball from studio to studio from the local, small time Out Of The Blue in Manchester's Ancoats to Olympic in Barnes to Loco Studios in Wales to the plush Monmow Studio's in Monmouth to London's Matrix to, eventually, Sawmills Studio's in Cornwall.

These sessions would be tainted by squabbling and recording naiveté, although it must be stated that, when the band finally wrenched themselves clear of the shadow of a producer, and Noel Gallagher took control – at Sawmills in Cornwall – many of the basic tracks that would eventually become their début album, *Definitely Maybe*, were laid onto tape inside ten days.

Initially the band had agreed to work with ex-Sensational Alex Harvey Band man, David Batchelor, who seemed to share the same musical leanings as Noel. Together the pair would chat through a bewildering maze of musical references and obsessions, flicking their way though their almost identical record collections. It seemed to everyone involved that, yet again, Oasis had stumbled into a perfect – and to the record company, essential – band/producer partnership. The liaison seemed so promising until they gathered around the mixing desk where the age difference (Batchelor is in his mid-fifties), began to tell. Noel wanted his initial recordings to be spiced with youthful energy, more Sex Pistols than Beatles, and attempted to inject a little madness into the recordings.

"I'd be pissed," he told *Mojo*'s Mark Ellen, "and I'd be saying, 'Let's get a bit mad here, let's get really young and compress the shit out of this so that the speakers blow up.' He'd go, 'Nope, 'cos this is the way we done it in our day, son.' I'd say I'd want it to sound like an aeroplane taking off, and he'd say, 'Oh, you mean you want a Yamaha Backwards Fucking Flange-Loop-Snubble with a Dirk on it?'"

Obviously, this was a generation gap that couldn't easily be fixed. Eventually, the role of producer fell to Gallagher himself, together with Mark Coyle, his old mate from his time with Inspiral Carpets.

The confusing mess that shrouded the early recordings of Oasis was indicated by the choice of sleeve for their first genuine, single release, 'Supersonic'. The photo depicted the band, mid-studio session, standing among wires and gadgetry within the softly lit Monmow Studios during sessions that were eventually scrapped in favour of the latter day manic surge that took place at Sawmills.

The sleeve was important, as it set the tone for a wave of covers that soon began to attract the kind of attention previously reserved for the retro portraits which had adorned The Smiths' singles. The images were the result of a collaboration between Art Director Brian Cannon and photographer Michael Spencer Jones. Cannon had worked from an office in the same New Mount Street complex as Inspiral Carpets, The Fall and latterly Oasis, and met Noel during his Inspirals period, although the pair hadn't spoken until Noel discovered that Cannon had been designing the artwork for Verve. He mentioned that he would need a good designer for his own band, although Cannon hardly took the proposition seriously until requested to attend the band in session in Monmouth.

The recordings coincided with the band's first press-scrutinised gigs, including their début appearance in London, at 'Water Rats' in Kings Cross, where a queue of curious folk swelled beyond the club's capacity, causing 200 to be turned away. Although apparently not the most intense gig of their early days, it was still tightly packed and uncomfortable enough to eventually rank alongside the Sex Pistols infamous 'Screen On The Green' appearance in Islington or, perhaps, The Smiths at the tiny and unspectacular Rock Garden.

The crowd was probably attracted by the steady tide of press reports depicting a band with a 'hooligan heart'. The ferocious sibling rivalry contained within Oasis had often been misconstrued as negative in-fighting and was all too soon complimented with the expected, and deserved, tales of hedonistic excess.

This minor press frenzy would reach a new level on February 18, 1994, when the band clambered onto a ferry at Harwich, bound for a support spot to Verve in Amsterdam. For the band, if for nobody else, the gig and the trip were events worthy of heady celebration and Liam and Guigs duly obliged by popping open a series of champagne bottles and spicing the fizz with an endless series of Jack Daniels 'slammers'. Inevitably, the session spilled over into a series of arguments and scuffles with fellow passengers, including a fearsome rabble of Chelsea fans. Tables and chairs crashed to the floor and following a fairly juvenile session of surging down the gangways, the pair were cornered, handcuffed and locked in the brig. There was more trouble, too, with Bonehead who was apprehended for 'causing a disturbance' following the mysterious ransacking of his cabin, while Tony McCarroll was detained for loudly banging on cabin doors. As the ferry disembarked in Holland, only a disgruntled Noel Gallagher could be seen striding onto the quayside.

The incident saw the cancellation of the Amsterdam gig and for the first time the rivalry between the two brothers made banner headlines. Liam, apparently, believed the incident to be

"...A great crack...very rock 'n' roll!" Noel, however, strongly disagreed. "It wasn't fucking rock 'n' roll at all. Rock 'n' roll is going to Amsterdam, blowing the audience away with a storming gig and coming back triumphant...not getting thrown off the ferry like some scouse schlepper with handcuffs. That's just football hooliganism...just fucking pathetic in my view. I felt pretty ashamed...Liam can be such a fucking prat, sometimes."

On a more positive note, the band's appearance on *The Word*, in March, served to effectively silence the cynics who had been bleating about the band being "Roses copyists". Performing 'Supersonic', they effectively demolished the in-studio opposition – a rather tepid Soul Asylum – and Noel took great delight in slagging off both the receding rave scene and the barrage of bands adopting a 'new punk' stance.

Defending the Oasis tendency to openly relate to 'old' music, he claimed in the *NME* "These bands that claim to be punk rock, they've just totally missed the point. They're all going on about The Clash and slogans and taking speed and all that, but they are all dead uptight about it. For me, punk rock was the Sex Pistols and they were big time fun. They covered Small Faces and Chuck Berry and Johnny Rotten, the Pistols were a fucking laugh and that's what it's all about." Portentously, he added, "and all we've got to say to Blur is Bleuuuuurgh!"

On *The Word*, Oasis did nothing to dispel the thick 'laddish' aura that had been hovering around them during the past few months. A lippy Liam opined that Paula Yates, also on the show that night, "was up for a bit of sorting out". This rather mild boast was complimented by the sight of Bonehead grabbing *Word* presenter Hufty, mouthing the words, "What are you into birds for, anyway?," before, rather disgustingly, licking the top of her head.

*   *   *

'Supersonic', the band's hyped-up début single was, astonishingly, recorded and mixed in less than eight hours. Had a larger record company been in charge, had a black-Levi clad A & R man from one of the major labels been overseeing the recordings, and reporting back to his company via a plethora of pointless meetings, then the track would have almost certainly remained a demo, to be replaced, no doubt, by a smoother, softer, more apparently radio-friendly final version.

As such, with their very first release, Oasis cut straight through such bullshit with consummate ease. A lesson, undoubtedly, for record companies who allow studio costs to escalate into an unrecoupable nightmare, only to be presented with little more than a mush that only faintly resembles the initial idea. Noel Gallagher, perhaps leaning on his Inspirals experience, resolutely refused to allow his band to wander into that much travelled cul-de-sac.

Much has been read into the rather daft 'Supersonic' lyrics although, at the risk of demystification, it must be noted that, the sound engineer's liverish Rottweiler aside, they meant absolutely nothing. With the recording powering along, Noel found himself having to slot a few more words into place. He was duly shunted into the corner of the studio, armed with nothing other than a biro and rapidly diminishing bottle of gin. It took just one hour for him to return to the fray, significantly worse for wear, hardly able to believe the words on the page before him. "I thought, fucking hell, I'm a weird cunt, me," he would later confide to *Melody Maker*.

Modestly, the song touched No.31, before fading rather rapidly. Nevertheless, it seemed fitting that this increasingly argumentative bunch of reprobates should choose this, their breakthrough period, to produce arguably the finest gig of their short existence on the small venue circuit, and it seemed fitting that it should take place at the 100 Club in London's Oxford Street, the scene, two decades earlier, of the notoriously violent 100 Club Punk festival, during which John Beverley – then the drummer with Flowers Of Romance – famously attacked *NME* writer Nick Kent with a rusty bike chain. The blows did little harm, although the blood would gush spectacularly from Kent's face and, that night, Beverley was christened Sid Vicious by a giggling, cheekily evil John Lydon.

"I know exactly what happened in this place," stated Noel Gallagher that night. "I'm well aware of it...the history of it, the importance of it...I mean, on the one hand it was just a bunch of stupid kids getting pissed and having a laugh...but, then again, there was an energy that changed things...and a fucking great rock band. Look at us now...look at Liam...yeah, he's a fucking stupid kid, getting pissed and having a laugh and we...well, we are a fucking great rock band. It's parallels, isn't it, history repeating itself."

The parallels continued. The first of a multitude of *NME* double page spreads hinged on Liam Gallagher taking childish exception to a previous live review, penned by excitable *NME* hack, Johnny Cigarettes.

"I'll slap him round at the show," stated Liam.

"Shut up, man," replied Noel, "Shut up!"

Liam: "No, you shut up, if I ever meet the fucker, I'll slap him."

Noel: "You are talking shit,"

Liam: "I'll hit him with a bottle right in his kipper. I'll smash the fuck right out of him...(turning to Noel)...Let's fucking go then, you dick...let's have a fucking fight...I hate this bastard (Noel), and that's what it's all about. That's why we'll be the best band in the world, 'cos I fucking hate that twat there, and I hope one day there's a time when I can smash the fuck right out of him. With a fucking Rickenbacker, right on the nose...then he can do the same to me."

The Gallagher bust-up echoed similar scenes in the Pistols camp, whether it be Rotten warring with his band or manager Malcolm McLaren. But while hindsight supports the belief that the Pistols' infighting was largely contrived, there was little doubt that, at the time, Liam harboured genuine loathing for his brother.

"The thing is," Noel told the proudly puerile 'lad mag' *Loaded*, "Liam don't write no lyrics, he doesn't play any instruments, doesn't write nothing – so all he is required to do is stand there and sing and fucking look good. I think he gets pissed off by the fact that he doesn't actually do anything because he can't. I dunno, I think he just winds me up on purpose, the cunt."

It was around this time when the hard northern heads of Oasis first clashed with the Colchester smoothness of Blur, the band who would soon, if only in the media, be pitted against Oasis, their complete antithesis. It occurred following a mini press conference, held by the *NME*, to celebrate '10 years of Creation Records', which surrounded the Undrugged concert at the Royal Albert Hall. Liam, Noel, The Boo Radleys and Ride all gathered around an *NME* microphone and, rather drearily as it turned out, discussed the musical matters of the day. Far more interesting was the unofficial continuation of this meeting, in the ironically named Good Mixer pub, in Camden. Once inside, Liam came face to face with Graham from Blur and immediately started berating him, apparently for no other reason than the fact that Oasis, just a couple of day previously, had all agreed that they shared a furious communal loathing for the fairly innocuous 'southerners'.

The abuse continued until the entire entourage left the pub and visited The Camden Underworld. Before long the abuse reached a near violent level, and Liam was asked to leave. The Oasis gang tumbled messily from the club, with one Creation employee attempting to 'drop kick' a particularly vindictive bouncer.

During this period a more lasting personality split began to grow within the band itself. For some time drummer Tony McCarroll had found himself increasingly on the outside, if not the butt of, the band's bewildering in-jokes. On a number of occasions, Liam had even verbally 'turned on' the hapless drummer for little apparent reason. McCarroll's growing state of isolation grew worse and matters came to a head during an impromptu game of football after a soundcheck at the Old Trout venue in Windsor.

Promoter Phil Hanks told *Vox* magazine: "What got me was that they were playing football outside, with football on the radio on really loud. It was Sheffield Wednesday vs Everton, and nobody would pass the ball to Tony. In the end he was moaning so much someone just smashed the ball at him from about three feet away."

The rift would fester, with McCarroll increasingly pushed

onto the Oasis periphery, eventually to be replaced, post-'Some Might Say', by Alan White.

*   *   *

'Shakermaker', the band's second single – which began life back in The Boardwalk rehearsal room – was destined to become their weakest outing, although this writer remains rather fond of it, and it would see the band threatened with litigation by, of all people, the writers of a New Seekers hit. This wasn't in the least bit surprising, as 'Shakermaker' must rank as one of the most blatant 'steals' in rock history, or at least since The Jam allegedly remodelled The Beatles' Taxman' and named it 'Start'.

Noel Gallagher courageously utilised the soaring little melody previously known as 'I'd Like To Teach The World To Sing', once, of course, the universal theme tune of Coca Cola. Creation, fearing that Coca Cola might start legal proceedings, came within a whisker of pulling the single at the last moment but then it snapped, and sailed away, and all they could do was wait and hope. Just to rub it in, Oasis even implanted the line, "I'd like to buy the world a Coke" at gigs, and Noel Gallagher insisted that the line should stay. Creation, however, had other ideas, and the line had strangely dissolved by the time the single hit the streets.

Rip-off or not, 'Shakermaker' pumped directly into the charts at No.11, and provided the band with their first *Top Of The Pops* appearance, performing in front of the 'vortex' swirl backdrop, absurdly stolen from Salfordian stalwarts, The Fall. More audacity! The sleeve, produced by the Cannon and Spencer Jones partnership, was an hilarious depiction of artefacts and fixtures, melting into a room while an Oasis tape revolved on a tape machine. In a weak nod back to the days when The Beatles would deliberately install misleading references into their cover art, the room was filled with odd items – old film stars, daffodils – that had absolutely no meaning whatsoever but were obviously set up to instigate rumour and myth. A clever ploy and a second great Oasis sleeve.

The song's lyrics caused an embarrassing ripple of music press speculation but were about absolutely nothing, well, almost nothing. Sifting through references to 'Mr Soft' – the Cockney Rebel tune recently enlivened by a soft mint television advertising campaign – you might unearth the odd nod to, as Noel eloquently stated, "some guy charlied off his fucking 'ead."

The legend of Oasis on the road was cemented, ironically, on the day that Manchester United, the team they loathed more than any other, were crowned league champions for the second year running. On this less than celebratory occasion – at least in the eyes of Oasis – the band went wild in The Ibis, a nondescript Portsmouth hotel, following a crammed 'sold out' gig at the town's Wedgewood Rooms.

It was, by all accounts, a surreal night. After the gig, the band had been invited to a typically appalling student party. They returned, somewhat disappointed, to the hotel to find East 17 flitting in and out of the lift. "Are you Blur?" asked East 17, tactlessly, though apparently sincerely. "No, are you Take That?" came the brash reply, which was duly celebrated in a feature in the following week's *NME*. Indeed, the *NME*'s Simon Williams witnessed the sorry sight of a band truly on the rampage that night. They raided the un-manned bar, dived into the adjacent swimming pool, and fought – apparently with genuine violence – over a girl who had, it seemed, liaised with both the brothers. Most of the bar chairs ended up in the pool and not for the first – or last – time, Bad News style clichés began to haunt Oasis reportage.

Although this 'laddishness' might have seemed rather contrived, it amounted to little more than 'excitable-lads-on-the-road' syndrome. Nevertheless, as the reports began to scatter more and more entertainingly across the news and feature pages of the music press, and even started to trickle into the more adventurous tabloids, it seemed clear that Oasis were a record company PR dream: a full blown, out of control bad lad band, garbed in street scally-chic and wholly representative of their audience. It was the first time this had happened on an interesting scale since Happy Mondays had imploded horribly a couple of years previously. Now, all of a sudden, here was a band who fully represented the much maligned gangs who gather on street corners on Fridays nights, a band fully prepared to air their furious angst in public. Anti-PC, anti-camp, anti-fashion!

As Noel Gallagher perceptively noted in the *NME*: "It's like, if you get a band like Suede, and they write pretty decent music and all that, but Brett Anderson's lyrics are basically a cross between Bowie and Morrissey. I don't think some 16 year old on the dole is going to understand what he means by 'Animal Nitrate', or whatever. The thing about The Smiths is that Johnny Marr was a lad and you knew he was a rock 'n' roller, that's why I got into them. And I think that a lot of kids find Suede too intellectual, and while with Blur they don't understand all that stuff about sugary tea. But with Oasis, like the Roses and the Mondays, it's bottom line. Here's a guitar. Here's the songs, you have them. We are not preaching about 'ye olde England' or how it was in the sixties. We're not preaching about our sexuality, we're not telling the kids how to act."

The reasons for the rise of Oasis suddenly seemed so painfully obvious. The audience was already in place, simply screaming for something solid, believable, untaxing perhaps. Even the fact that Oasis stood stock still on stage – "I'd love to dance around but I have got to stand still and concentrate" claimed Noel Gallagher – fell heavily in their favour. This lack of physical exertion made them the complete antithesis, not just of the fey, wilting prancing of Morrissey and Brett Anderson, but also of the pretty boy bands, Take That and East 17. It was beginning to dawn on a lot of people that Oasis, no matter how hard they tried, just couldn't seem to put a foot wrong.

Noel Gallagher: "Music for me at the moment is dead. It's poncey and serious and everyone's gotta make some kind of a statement, whether it is about 'Parklife' or their feminine side or their politics. But we are a rock 'n' roll band – we say all you need is cigarettes and alcohol."

*   *   *

During the summer of 1994, Oasis threw themselves furiously into the role of a 'breaking band'. A mid-sized venue tour of Britain in May quickly sold out, while in June they all but dominated proceedings at the vastly improved Glastonbury Festival. Although their set had yet to bulge into something worthy of arena proportions, their nine songs – including 'I Am The Walrus', by this time a famously wacky encore – succeeded in barging their way onto the 'Channel 4 Goes To Glastonbury' programme.

It was the first time that television cameras had actually managed to penetrate to the heart of this vast festival, without seeming either indignant or patronising. Oasis, for their part, seemed only mildly phased by the open air event although some of their intensity did seem to evaporate into the hot summer skies. This, coupled with the natural dilution which occurs when live sets are transposed onto television, meant that it was a substantially weakened Oasis who graced late night television, at least on that occasion.

Noel Gallagher professed mixed feelings about the Glastonbury experience but the situation would be wholly rectified one year later when the band, blessed with a bigger sound and bigger stage presence, seized Glastonbury by the proverbial scruff of the neck, wringing out a furious set that was matched only by the awesome peak scaled by Pulp circa 'Common People'.

Noel had seemed more content three days earlier when he joined ex-Icicle Works frontman Ian McNabb on stage at London's Kings College. Backing them, and inducing in Gallagher a noticeable state of awe, were Ralph Molina and Billy Talbot of Neil Young's legendary backing band, Crazy Horse. They performed a furious version of the of Sky Saxon And The Seeds nugget 'Pushin' Too Hard', and Echo And The Bunnymen's early indie classic, 'Rescue'. This impromptu jam, perhaps the first solid indication that Noel Gallagher, unlike say the Sex Pistols, was perfectly willing to embrace rock 'n' roll history, was so successful that the two Crazy Horse musicians, excited at finding "the most extraordinary musicians in England", travelled to Manchester to catch an

Oasis gig just days later.

Not that Gallagher's task had exactly proved taxing. "Do you know 'Pushin' Too Hard'?" asked the Crazy Horse duo, "Er, I think so," muttered Gallagher, sarcastically, "What are the chords...A minor G...I think I can just about pull that off."

It was a little coup that had obviously delighted Gallagher, for he was soon to boast "My mum's dead proud of me, I have already had my picture taken with Arthur Lee (of Love), I've been on stage with Crazy Horse and I am going to have my picture taken with Johnny Cash. All I need now is my picture taken with Burt Bacharach and I've got the set." Pretty hip mum, eh! Not so for Liam...

"Our kid just wants to play with old cunts," was the younger brother's sole comment on the matter.

Noel's desire to link up with rock's historical hierarchy proved rather surprising. Traditionally, rock's burgeoning rebels, from the early Who to the Sex Pistols, had deemed it necessary to deride most that had gone before. Not Gallagher. Refreshingly, he also cared little for whatever the music press decided was hip.

A self-confessed U2 fan, he caught the band live at Sellafield, and rejoiced when they launched into versions of Abba's 'Dancing Queen' and Lou Reed's 'Satellite Of Love'. He even confessed to queuing up to purchase 'Achtung Baby' and sat in awe-struck silence as this most unusual album unfolded on his stereo. More disturbingly, he professed to be a Pink Floyd fan and even worse, believed the band's pompous 1979 epic, 'The Wall' to be their finest ever album.

Chatting openly, once again to *Mojo*'s Mark Ellen – who had perceptively hoisted the band onto a plateau that seemed rather high for their thin discography – Noel picked out a few songs he wished he had written. The list proved surprisingly disparate and highly significant.

"'Up The Hill Backwards' by David Bowie. Every single Beatles song. 'To Love Somebody' by The Bee Gees. Phenomenal band, The Bee Gees. 'Harry Braff' on the *Horizontal* album. 'SOS' by Abba, wish I'd written that. I used to love Split Enz. 'Don't Dream It's Over' by Crowded House would be a Desert Island Disc for me, I'm still trying to rip it off to this day. 'Car Trouble' by Adam And The Ants. 'Being Boiled' by The Human League. Weller. 'English Rose'. Kinks. Who. A few by U2. 'One' is possibly the most beautiful song ever written. I cried my fucking eyes out man. The feel, the emotion in his voice, it's heart-rending that song. I've got everything they have ever done."

Abba? Crowded House? Bee Gees? Two things seemed obvious here. Noel Gallagher harbours a profound and intelligent love of 'the song', and this triumphs over all kinds of ebbs and flows of hipness. No jumped up, post-grad, dumb rock journo could ever guide his listening habits one way or the other. How refreshing, perhaps, to see a new star refusing to introduce the world to slabs of obscure ska, or Germanic avant-garde warbling, or fearsome Chicago blues. No John Coltrane or Woody Guthrie or Augustos Pablo in that list. No Joy Division, Smiths, Fall or Velvet Underground either. Noel Gallagher was obviously not a man overflowing with hip references. Nobody ever expected him to pledge devotion to Camus, Satre or even Kerouac, Burroughs or Waits, but to pluck such influences, all of which could be found languishing dustily in any parental record collection, was simply unprecedented. By comparison, a love of Sky Saxon And The Seeds seems positively anarchic.

*   *   *

Further 'on-the-road' antics darkened the summer of '94, with the band trashing their room at The Columbia at Marble Arch which promptly banned them. This is London's celebrated rock biz hotel and not an easy institution to be ejected from, though The Fall once managed it after Brix Smith absent-mindedly left a bath running and went out on the town. Nevertheless, until Oasis arrived, practically every hedonistic band in the world had failed to unhinge the normally unshockable Columbia staff.

In Sweden, Oasis, in league with Verve, managed to get themselves banned from the country following a spate of chair-chucking and ripping telephones from their sockets. That particular hotel landed the two bands with identical bills for £1,000 in damages.

Some things are simply meant to be - it would be futile to resist. If you told Liam and Noel Gallagher in July 1994 that within eighteen months they would have conquered America, they would surely have looked towards you in a state of disbelief. "Eighteen months?" one of them, almost certainly Liam, would ask. "How come it would take so long?"

Eighteen months, of course, is a mere flicker in America's eye although perhaps it wouldn't have seemed so, that night in July 1994, when Oasis made their US début in New York, during the much loathed and drunkenly celebrated New Music Seminar, an annual four-day ritual of frightening rock biz sycophancy which by day takes place in the lush conference suites of the New York Hilton and by night in Manhattan's multitudinous small venues. Oasis wouldn't have been aware of this, but the sheer audacious flash and verve of the New Music Seminar – very much the blueprint for Manchester's 'In The City' event – was traditionally blessed by two extremes: ambitious US acts on the make, blatantly eager to impress the music industry bods, and surly, distant English acts, solidly determined to do precisely the opposite.

Whether this English arrogance serves our bands well or not remains open to question but it is certainly relevant to note that, just as Oasis were pricking painfully into America's eastern edge, Suede, originally touted as being the next big thing from England, had already been shunted into the small pockets of America's underground where they could do little harm. Oasis made it immediately clear that they had no intention of performing to a few spotty oiks in Seattle, Chicago and LA. They wanted 'in', big style and initially those manning the American industry machine just stood laughing.

On the band's very first night in America, a bunch of industry executives from Sony whisked the sullen band off to dinner. After just one hour, one of them informed the upstart named Liam that they should be grateful to be represented by such an important label. Incensed, Liam told them that it was the other way around, and promptly left for a gig.

The incident was minor but dangerous. Liam probably didn't realise just how many acts have scuppered their chances by taking such actions. Was it Liam Gallagher marking out his territory, trampling over the bullshit, or merely refusing to intelligently accept the status quo? Perhaps a bit of both. As it turned out, it did the band no harm at all.

This initial foray into the US saw the band closing ranks even more than usual, adopting a furious 'us and them' mentality despite the money that Sony was spending on them, and this attitude was surely heightened further by the close proximity of the New Music Seminar. America was the enemy. It had to be defeated.

Curiously enough, the band, including prime hotel room trasher Bonehead, were uncharacteristically well behaved during their New York stay. Nevertheless, there was an entertaining little affray which took place in the presence of *Melody Maker*'s Paul Mathur – a perceptive early champion of the Oasis cause – in the band's hotel foyer. Apparently an outspoken American guest, taking exception to the band's boundless braggadocio, voiced the opinion that, "...there's no way you lot will make it in America." Berating Liam, his pony tail flapping behind him, he pledged an allegiance to 'real' bands, like Pearl Jam, Nirvana and, most curiously, The Soup Dragons.

"Listen man!" replied Liam testily, "don't you ever tell me that what I do doesn't mean anything because I can do things you can't even dream about. I'll steal your soul and you won't even notice it. I've stolen it now while you were standing there...and don't talk to me about Nirvana. He was a sad cunt who couldn't handle the fame. We're stronger than that. And you can fuck off with your fucking Pearl Jam."

This moment would be destined to sink into Oasis folklore, and it is easy to forget that at the time of this little verbal explosion, Oasis were little more than one of a small barrage of British bands all hoping to break through in a big way.

Oasis made their US début at the city's Wetlands venue. Reluctance to play the American industry game aside, the band understood that it was quite possibly the most important gig they had played since Alan McGee had stumbled across them in Glasgow. Had they imploded into a mess of surliness, which can happen when the mood doesn't suit them, they might well have blown their American chance at the very first obstacle. As it was, they raised their game, finishing triumphantly with 'I Am The Walrus'.

A nice, comic touch was provided by Blondie's Jimmy Destri who, after witnessing the band's proud cliché strewn set and hearing that Noel Gallagher was ready to rip off Blondie's 'Hanging On The Telephone', handed over a note with the relevant chord sequence scrawled across it. "Steal these and we'll find you!" the note said.

"He's just scared we'll do it better," laughed Noel.

Despite their celebrated frostiness, the band – all of them – secretly confided to Paul Mathur that they had all but fallen in love with the industry machine and their part in it, especially in America. Although Noel, of course, had been there before with the Inspirals, he had never before felt the full power of the industry swelling beneath his feet. For Liam and the rest of the band, the total experience was both new and intoxicating.

"I fucking love this, me," confessed Liam, "Love it...not just us, but America. I can't believe it, it's a wonderful place and we can't fail to completely conquer it...what an adventure! Our kid was always going on about what U2 did in the States and I always thought it was a load of tosh, all that. You know, just a big commercial thing...but it must have been amazing for them...and here we are at the other side of that adventure. Just think, there are all these kids in these little towns all across the States and they are all gonna be into us. I don't care if that sounds egotistical...it fucking is egotistical...and this is probably turning me head...but fuck it, it's bound to turn me head a bit...can't wait to get back over here...don't want to go back to Manchester!"

With the new single 'Live Forever' pending, the chance to use the Stateside sojourn to film a video was eagerly snapped up. Director Carlos Grasso, the man responsible for Grant Lee Buffalo's 'Fuzzy' video, was brought into the frame to suggest a few innovatory video ideas that worried the somewhat bewildered band. A couple of inserts, for instance, would see Liam being nailed in a chair on a 20 foot high wall, Bonehead would be drowned in a shower and Tony buried alive – significantly, perhaps – in Alphabet City. Perhaps closer to the heart of Oasis would be the filming of a mock performance in the middle of the night on a bandstand in the centre of Central Park. This hugely illuminated show – fittingly within spitting distance of the Dakota building, outside which John Lennon was shot – drew a riotous assembly of disparate tramps, flick-knife gangs, druggies, alcoholics and brave or foolhardy rock fans, all of whom were treated to acoustic versions of 'Live Forever', 'Cigarettes And Alcohol' and 'Listen Up'. Had Liam had his way, following the video shoot a full PA would have been hastily assembled and a full gig would have taken place, no doubt to be swiftly halted by the NYPD, already circulating with intent. Noel, however, thought the idea ludicrous.

"Elvis fucking Presley doesn't want to do it," mocked Liam, "That's why he's a cunt and I hate him. Look at this, a gig would be great, fuck the video, fuck the seminar, fuck New York...Let's just do it now!"

CHAPTER SIX
Definitely...Maybe

The release of Oasis' phenomenal début album – destined to become the fastest selling début long player in the history of the British charts – was preceded by 'Live Forever', featuring a Rottenesque whine about, in Noel Gallagher's words, "having a friend who could be your friend for life. The lyrics are saying that I don't care about your bad points, I love you for the good in you."

Very occasionally an album comes along that redefines the current state of music. Beneath it, everything else has to reshuffle, every band has to take stock, explore their faults, and start again. *Definitely Maybe* was so simple in many ways, and so obvious, and so perfect that there would be little more to say. Other bands might slag it off as a knee-jerk reaction but even the most insular musician would recognise effortless superiority when they heard it. Worse still, the 'fans' of these lesser bands would hear it also, and it only took one listen to realise that Oasis had finally delivered, in effect, the second great Stone Roses album. Here it was, no doubt about it. The real second coming, and British rock would never be quite the same again.

The album opened with 'Rock 'n' Roll Star', written by Noel after he'd watched The Rolling Stones run through 'Brown Sugar' on BBC 2's *Sounds Of the Eighties*, a vision which reminded him of his childhood dreams of becoming a rock star. In *Melody Maker*, Noel Gallagher would state "I hope that when people put this album on in years to come there will be some kid bouncing around the bedroom with a tennis racket to 'Rock 'n' Roll Star'."

About 'Shakermaker', Noel said: "I'll go on the record here as saying it's got fuck all to do with the New Seekers...it's more of a rip off of 'Flying' by The Beatles than anything else". The other single 'Live Forever' was followed by 'Up In The Sky', a basic put down of rock biz icons. Gallagher: "It's basically about people who think they are the voice of a generation, or the figurehead or movement. It's just saying, 'Why are you lot looking up at him?'"

Listening to 'Up In The Sky', one tends to think of Noel Gallagher lugging the Inspiral Carpets gear on to the stage for the 500th time, or sitting in their office answering the telephones, confused by the knowledge that the band he had just joined, who couldn't seem to attract more than three people and a dog into The Boardwalk, were simply in a different musical league.

'Columbia', the first song that Oasis ever played live, is an affectionate nod towards the dance music that dominated those increasingly distant days. It was followed by the mighty, fresh sounding 'Supersonic', and the ragged punk howl of 'Bring It On Down', another reactionary title coupling a Sex Pistols sneer with an existential theme. 'Cigarettes And Alcohol' was a most welcome hymn to hedonism - get pissed kid, 'ave a fag. If the riff is nicked from T Rex, then perhaps the steal is most fitting, for T. Rex were the ultimate unpretentious, good time teen band, although Noel quite rightly stated: "Yeah...of course I nicked it from Bolan...but he swiped it from Howlin' Wolf and nobody would ever have begrudged him."

'Digsy's Dinner' is, and will remain, one of the strangest concepts, an ode to a mate of Noel's, 'Digsy', who still plays in Liverpool band Small. When Digsy once rather innocently asked Noel round for tea, arranged to pick him up at three o'clock and offered him some lasasgne, little did he know that he had just written three lines from one of the finest rock albums of all time. "I think it's the most English song on the album," stated Noel. "It's like The Small Faces meet the Kinks meet Oasis."

'Sad Song', another oddity, written by Noel late one night after a vinyl pressing problem had made it necessary to slot in another song, remains perhaps the album's oddest track. A downer, even defeatist piece, 'Sad Song' is about the simplification of fate, it happens or it doesn't. After Noel had played an acoustic run through of the song on Radio 1's *Evening Session*, the disembodied voice of a tearful Alan McGee filtering through a mobile phone informed Noel that, "Noel, fucking hell, it's the best song ever written. I'm sitting here crying, you bastard, you are the bastard son of John Lennon!"

According to Noel, 'Slide Away', written while briefly smitten, will remain the only love song he will ever write. He'll be briefly smitten again, of that there is little doubt, and more lilting love melodies will surely emerge. 'Married With Children' was written while Noel was watching the TV show of the same name, wallowing in the kind of reflection which that particular sit-com tends to throw up. The song is about pettiness, the squabbles that fester in any live-in relationship.

"That's why we put it after 'Slide Away' because 'Slide Away' is an uplifting song about two people in love and after it comes the cynical thing where they've moved in with each other, they're married with children and they fucking hate each other."

*   *   *

Released on August 30, 1994, *Definitely Maybe* wasted little time in breaking records. Within three days of issue, the ferocity of the initial sale astonished everyone apart from Noel Gallagher, as a massive 150,000 flew across the counters in the UK, pumping the album directly to No.1 Although the preceding hype, which had been considerable, had suggested such a thing, the record industry was still rather stunned, especially as Oasis competed with a £2 million television advertising campaign for 'The Three Tenors', Carrreras, Domingo and Pavarotti, who had all but booked their place at the top.

Even on the day of its release it seemed that something rather special was happening. At the Marble Arch branch of the Virgin Megastore, over 1,000 fans crammed onto the pavement to attempt to force their way into the store to catch the band running through an almost impromptu acoustic set comprising of songs from the album. Unfortunately, as licensing laws would only allow 200 into the store, tension raged around the shop's entrance.

Those unable to squeeze inside missed Oasis running cheerily through their three singles, plus 'Sad Song', 'Slide Away' and the forthcoming hit, 'Whatever'. The latter song featured an unexpected guest appearance by Evan Dando, of Lemonheads fame, who claimed that after meeting the band the previous evening in Holland he'd had written a song with Gallagher called 'Purple Parallelogram'.

CHAPTER SEVEN
Hedonism And Acrimony

The swift ascendancy of the band and their fan base, which seemed to be swelling on a daily basis, can perhaps be attributed to the unusually high element of 'incident' that seemed to dog their live shows throughout the summer. Promoters, unable to keep pace with the increased security problems as small venues became stretched to capacity and beyond, found it difficult to maintain full control. The upside of this situation meant that Oasis gigs were unusually intense affairs, heightened by the fact that the band had already transcended the mid-size hall circuit. But there were problems.

In Newcastle, on the very first date of their British tour, violence erupted in the hall and soon spilled out of the Riverside venue and into the surrounding streets. The catalyst for this outbreak was one mindless 'fan' who clambered drunkenly on to the stage, punched Noel Gallagher in the face, narrowly missing his eye, and staggered back into the crowd. Those stage-side were stunned further when Liam and Noel jumped into the 500 strong crowd in hot pursuit of the attacker.

Radio 1's Jo Whiley, who was at the gig, later stated: "The guy who punched Noel had a huge ring on his finger. Noel had loads of blood pouring down his face. It was awful. Very scary. People were trying to get backstage and were throwing bottles at the crew."

The violence failed to subside and a crowd of over 300 gathered around the band's van, smashing windows until eventually, it sped off, only to collide with a VW Golf.

Apparently the crowd, more akin to the terraces of the seventies than a nineties rock gig, fell ingloriously into puerile football chants such as, "Soft as shite" and more provocatively,

"Man City wank...wank...wank!"

Perhaps it was no coincidence that the attack took place during the band's punk anthem, 'Bring It On Down'.

"I just looked up from my guitar and this guy was leering before me," stated Noel, "and I just thought he was a stage diver, then I clocked this big ring on his finger and he just smacked me...I've got a bit of a headache...there is a lump gathering over my eye but if I have another 75 cigarettes and a couple of bottles of gin, I'll be sort of alright...I might get to sleep tonight."

Later, Noel put forth a curious theory. "I blame the strobe lights. We decided to get a lighting engineer for this tour, and we told him, we don't want strobe lights because we can't see what we are doing when they are on. So he said, 'Right' and he just put them on during the drum for the beginning of 'Bring It On Down' and all hell broke loose."

Liam Gallagher, unusually reflective that night, admitted: "We are prime targets for dickheads, aren't we? We have this stupid 'hard man' reputation. People think we are up for a fight and that, but we're not up for a fight. We didn't start it. We are here to play songs, that's what we are about. We are not about fighting...we want to do the set and get off...but if someone gets on stage and wants to have a go then they are going to get it. I can't understand the mentality of a guy who wants to pay money to go into a gig and smack one of the band. I feel sorry for all those people who paid money to go to that gig. The thing is it sets a precedent and it won't happen again. We've been saying for a year to our record company and our manager that we need more security and it's all, 'We can't afford it'. But does it take someone to lose an eye to get security?"

Although security was duly stepped up following the incident, it seems significant to note that Noel Gallagher continued to feel distraught. Not for his eye, but for the damage inflicted on his guitar, a vintage Gibson Les Paul sunburst, once the property of Pete Townshend and given to him by Johnny Marr.

Suddenly it seemed that a certain instability had become in-built at Oasis gigs, be it a result of an over-zealous audience, or under par band. The chances of an Oasis gig running smoothly, without chaos, sporadic violence or on-stage bickering seemed remote and certainly added a certain frisson to the proceedings.

By the time the band returned to America – following swift and heady trips to Europe and Japan – chaos had broken out again after Noel allegedly quit the band following yet another bust up with his brother. He did a vanishing act after a series of shows in California, and subsequent gigs in Dallas, Kansas and Missouri had to be cancelled. Later, Noel was spotted drifting through the casinos of Las Vegas, apparently wholly unconcerned about the state of the band he had departed, albeit temporarily. The official explanation for this apparent 'split' was that Oasis were suffering from "gig exhaustion", and they had all been given time to cool off before re-grouping in Austin, Texas.

Despite this officially harmonious split, it was with some relief that the band welcomed Noel back into their ranks to continue the tour and record B-sides at a local studio. Indeed, despite Noel's insistence that, "yeah, it was a split, so what...I just got fuckin' sick of them...especially our kid. I just wanted to chill out for a while," the band fell into a full and heady schedule including their recording of an 'Unplugged' special for MTV, but there was a good deal more to it than that.

It happened, as it so often does, in Los Angeles. If you are an English rock act drifting through or conquering Los Angeles, you will almost certainly find yourself in a restaurant on Sunset Boulevard sharing a meal with infamous KROQ DJ and professional Anglophile Rodney Bingenheimer, a pixie-ish socialite who since the mid-sixties has known and partied everyone who has ever had anything to do with the LA rock scene. Never one to spurn the chance of latching onto a hot new act, Bingenheimer was present when Oasis signed to Sony and, as ever, he immediately ingratiated himself with the band.

Naturally, they agreed to go on Rodney's programme when they were in LA. Without perhaps quite knowing what they had let themselves in for, they also agreed to appear on a ludicrous KROQ phone-in-come-problem-page affair. Noel and Bonehead duly obliged and found themselves confronted with all manner of LA loonies, all suffering from the weirdest and most contrived problems one could possibly think of. This little ordeal – too much really, for an exhausted, jet lagged band to cope with – could easily have thrown them off track, but they seemed to cope admirably, dispensing northern common-sense and biting sarcasm in equal measure, little of which was recognised by the dauntingly humourless callers.

All seemed well, albeit superficially. Underneath, however, the cracks were beginning to grow in the band's celebrated resolve. The situation, a result of too much work, too much success perhaps, and too soon, was probably summed up in the wise words of manager Marcus Russell, who warned them about the perils of America.

"In Britain, a band is like a dinghy," he stated, "but in America, once you get the thing moving, it's like a ship...it is just so hard to stop and so easy to lose control." For a while, in Los Angeles, the lads lost control of the ship, and it almost, almost ran dangerously aground. They had been playing gig after gig, night after night and for some reason the entire logistics of gigging became confused. Even fundamental things went curiously wrong. None of the band even had the same set list. Noel's set list, rather bizarrely, was over six months old. Hence, the music would begin and crumble to a halt, with each band member looking around in confusion.

The professionalism that had typified Oasis had simply drained away, helped perhaps by the fact that most of the band hadn't slept for over 48 hours. One gig, quite the worst they had ever played – and they knew it – was witnessed, alas, by Ringo Starr. Not that Starr noticed the band's lack of cohesion. He exited the gig singing their praises. Unlike Noel Gallagher. In the dressing room he gave the other members a roasting.

"If you don't want to do this," he told them, "if you are not going to put everything you've got into it, if you are going to fuck around, then do it when we've finished the band. We'll have time to do it then. But right now I only want to be in a group that wants to do something."

The band, reeling with indignation, failed to respond, so Noel decided to split up the group there and then. With $800 tour money in his hand, and an ounce of coke in his pocket, he got on the first available plane at LA airport. In his head, he was on his way back to England. In actuality, he stopped off at Vegas before continuing to San Francisco. From there he eventually hopped in a cab, wholly intent on booking himself back to the UK and finishing the band for good.

Then he found himself skimming through a copy of *Melody Maker*, only for his eyes to water at the sight of a couple of Oasis 'Sold Out' gig adverts. Although he didn't even know the band were supposed to be playing them – he had long since lost track of the itinerary – he wondered about the people who had bought tickets. As condescending as it may sound, Noel Gallagher knew he would have to return to the band and sort it out.

"Honestly," he told *Melody Maker*'s Paul Mathur. "After that gig I really didn't want to be in Oasis any more. It had been building up for weeks and then it just came to a head. I couldn't see any good coming out of carrying on. What was happening was the complete opposite of the reason why we started the band in the first place. We were all getting caught up in a lot of madness."

And so the American adventure continued, an unholy rigmarole of record company receptions – "So tell me about this Brit Pop thing, guys?" – and evening gigs. For Oasis, as for any band, their first solid exposure to America was proving to be a massive shock, a learning process. Would they survive? Somewhat concerned, the third Gallagher brother, Paul, turned up Stateside, surrounded by a small legion of 'Burnage boys' and the seemingly omnipresent Paul Mathur. (Bizarrely, Paul Gallagher actually applied for a job in the marketing department of Sony USA, and even turned up for the interview. During the interview, however, Noel walked into the office and heard Paul talking, "about how he could increase margins and stuff. I told them to throw him right out. Jeezus, he's an unemployed labourer from Burnage!"

Despite the rumours of 'hiccups', most of the British contingent fully expected to see Oasis soaring to Stateside success with full throttle performances, but the band that strolled on to the stage on the first night, like a bunch of reluctant schoolboys forced to attend a religious instruction class, fell rather short of expectations. The tension within the ranks was strikingly evident. All of the members appeared to be playing with sneering aloofness. At one point, an unusually apologetic Marcus Russell turned to Mathur and said: "You just don't want to know what has gone on...you just don't want to know!"

Things improved towards the end of the gig, presumably because of the unlikely Manchester City 'in jokes' that came from the Mancunian contingent. Suddenly the band, sensing that they were among friends at last, seemed to rediscover their fervour. 'Cigarettes And Alcohol' apparently saw them soaring back, albeit very briefly, to a peak. This resolve was cemented at the band's final date of the tour, a wholly triumphant return to New York's Wetlands. It was a vital performance, rather like a Carling Premiership six pointer. It was a gig that Oasis simply had to win.

Noel Gallagher: "Oh boy...that was a classic. One of the best gigs ever...and it had to be, didn't it? If we had gone out with a whimper, I don't know whether we would have survived, it was that close. But the gig was all the better because of what had gone on before. We knew that we came very close to splitting up...and for good, prior to that gig and yet we managed to turn it around, which was very satisfying. It was a gig that showed Oasis as exactly what they are meant to be. Something positive out of the negative...that's the whole point....and, despite all the shit, the tour has still been good. Playing little places, in the south or wherever, and all the kids knew all the words...they had been listening on college radio." ('Live Forever', incidentally, remained at No.1 on the college circuit throughout the tour).

*   *   *

Early Oasis (l-r): Liam, Guigsy, Bonehead, McCarroll, Noel

Oasis, 1994

Liam, New Cross Venue, 1994

Clockwise: Noel, Guigsy, Liam

Tony McCarroll and replacement Alan White

Above: Liam with Bonehead

Below: Lord Noel of Glastonbury and Liam playing ball

Liam, Vancouver, 1996

Working class guitar hero?

In November, 1994, 120,000 people crammed into Barcelona's Nou Camp to witness the home side rip apart Manchester United, though it seemed with the current state of English club football that a 4-0 score line hardly flattered the victors. In Manchester, people were either weeping or celebrating. Oasis certainly weren't weeping. Neither were they in Manchester. At 5am the following morning, they were staggering along Paris' Rue Amiral Duperre, locked in triumphant song. Locked also in the kind of warped glory that descends upon the followers of Manchester City every time their illustrious neighbours slip up, major style.

It may seem sad to note, but this was the best night in Manchester City's history since they demolished United 5-1 before the nineties had officially got under way. The residents of Paris really should have allowed the band a little space, a little freedom to run and wreck and scream down the avenues, bouncing into the Peugeots and Renaults, acting like the perennial English football thugs. Eventually, the band would tumble back into the foyer of the Amiral Duperre Hotel, much to the barely-contained disgust of the hotel staff, who had seen some rock stars in their time, but no one had ever, surely, been quite as awkward, arrogant, dismissive and downright obnoxious as this crew. By the time the band left the next day – temporarily minus Noel Gallagher, who caused no end of panic by drifting out alone into the Paris streets – the Hotel made a pledge, which they circulated around the local hotel circuit, that never again would they put their staff through that kind of ordeal.

Oasis were in Paris as part of a Britpop package, put together by the French rock magazine *Les Inrockuptibles,* a three night extravaganza spread across four cities, Lyon, Marseilles, Lille and Paris which also featured Echobelly, Gene, Elastica and Shed Seven. Top billing was shared by Oasis and Echobelly. Those expecting a show of British camaraderie would have been somewhat disappointed, especially when faced with the sheer aloofness and belligerence of Oasis.

Shed Seven's Rick Witter later told the *NME*: "We get on with most people, but Oasis, they were here last night and Noel won't even look at us when he's talking. We're like, 'Alright, how's it going?' and he just looks the other way and goes, 'Alright, 'cept there's lots of shit groups playing these gigs.' And you know who he's talking about. He was acting like a right pop star."

Although most bands tend to get along just fine, the animosity between Shed Seven and Oasis seemed to fester rather nastily, though Noel would hint that it wasn't merely one way traffic.

"We've been doing the same shows, the same interviews as Shed Seven, only they were a day ahead of us. In every interview we had the journalists saying, 'Oooh, we spoke to Shed Seven and they really took the piss out of you.' Well...what happens is we then bump into the band and they are dead matey, asking us how it is going, what we make of Paris...it's embarrassing. Slag us off but don't make small talk as well, life's too short...it's not as if they are any good. They may be liked by the French people, but there are loads of English who have travelled to see us. You can't expect people to travel to see that crap, can you? Who would do that?"

Back in England in December, the gigs that preceded the release of the mighty new single 'Whatever' were typically blighted by incident. At Glasgow Barrowlands, the gig was effectively cut short when Liam punched his mike stand and strode sullenly offstage after his voice had failed after just two unusually ragged songs. During 'Rock 'n' Roll Star', Liam rasped and gasped like an aged Tom Waits – leaving the band to chunder through 'Up In The Sky' before casting sheepish glances at each other. Noel, summoning up a modicum of control, assured the crowd that "We will go and see if we can sort this out," before returning five minutes later to state: "I'm sorry, his voice has gone, there is nothing we can do."

After the inevitable swell of consternation rippled dangerously around the ever volatile Glasgow crowd, Noel Gallagher returned and, ignoring the rather disarming chorus of 'Flower Of Scotland', courageously attempted a solo set. Although this served to placate half the crowd, the remainder began to growl menacingly. According to the Creation Press office, Noel's set was greeted with "rapturous applause" though *Melody Maker* correspondent Calvin Bush later described it as "muted". Had the gig finished there and then a riot might well have ensued. Sensing this, Noel walked back on stage with the band in tow. Ignoring cries of "Liam is a wanker" the band, with Noel singing, performed 'Shakermaker', 'Supersonic', 'Slide Away' and 'I Am The Walrus' before the house lights dissolved the atmosphere. The jeering which followed was eventually quelled by the sight of the promoter bravely walking on stage and promising a free gig at Christmas for anyone retaining their ticket stubs.

CHAPTER EIGHT
I'll Sing The Blues
If I Want

There were lighter moments during this period. Noel Gallagher had temporarily moved into Johnny Marr's Hale Barns home, and it was with Marr that Gallagher realised another dream, the chance to 'get kitted up' and blast a ball into the net at Maine Road. "It was the first time I'd been on the pitch without the police chasing me off it," he admitted, although his performance in a rock 'n' celeb charity kick about saw him whack the ball towards a gaping goal mouth, only to see it ricochet off the post and out into the stand.

Liam fared little better, falling head over heels after he stubbed his foot horribly into the ground, missing the goal from a distance of just one yard. "Well, what the fuck do you expect...we are Man City fans?" he later explained. His antics caused a good degree of hilarity from the players who assembled around him, including The Cult's Mancunian guitar slinger Billy Duffy.

The Oasis/Manchester City connection was growing, and had begun to surface on the terraces where – much to the band's delight – there were a number of passing Oasis references in City's infamously self-deprecatory chants. A year later, the band would even become potential team sponsors. The team has a long list of pop star patrons as City have always been regarded as the poorer but 'hipper' half of the Manchester football equation despite such United followers as Mick Hucknall, Terry Hall, Morrissey and Factory Records boss Tony Wilson.

Pop star involvement at City director level was constantly mooted, though surprisingly never quite finalised, during the team's most recent dark ages. M People's Mike Pickering, Rick

68

Wakeman, Mike And The Mechanics singer Paul Young and the managers of Simply Red and New Order, all Maine Road regulars, were constantly linked, if only in the local press, as potential investors. Oasis immediately made it known that they would be more than happy to join that pack. Liam Gallagher, casting his mind back a mere two years, boasted about his sacking from a dodgy car valeting job after he had "chucked a bucket of water over Ryan Giggs."

The only surprising aspect of this was that he hadn't been sacked earlier. Like the time, for instance, that he "wire wooled" Paul Ince's BMW and scratched Cantona's Audi. Not that such incidents deterred Giggs, a couple of years later, from telephoning a venue in an attempt to blag some Oasis tickets. His call was directed straight to Noel Gallagher who surprised nobody by replying, "No way, you must be joking, you can fuck off!"

*   *   *

Noel Gallagher had been boasting about his new song 'Whatever' for months. "We've got a song coming...a big one...a really big one...in fact it's the greatest song ever written," he immodestly proclaimed to an assembled row of sundry hacks back in mid-94. Few of them held their breath, for such statements were becoming alarmingly commonplace. The fact that nobody could genuinely claim that he ever fell short of his own promises still couldn't disguise the fact that such intense self congratulation can be wearying and rather pointless. Nevertheless, if it is a residue of supreme confidence, as would seem to be the case, then it's a small price to pay.

'Whatever', when it finally arrived, probably wasn't the greatest song ever, but probably was the greatest song of 1994 (it just sneaked into '94, courageously released for the last singles chart of the year on December 19). It was, undeniably, a 'big' song, and grander still, thanks to the soaring Abbey Road style orchestration. Although it was prevented from grasping the Christmas No.1 slot, beaten down by East 17 and the dreaded Mariah Carey, it was probably the song that edged the

69

band towards an older audience. It immediately took up residence on the adult rock Virgin Radio station, slotting neatly and lucratively alongside the likes of Bruce Springsteen, U2, Mike And The Mechanics and Sheryl Crow.

This nurturing of an older fan base was helped by a superb appearance on the excellent *Later With Jools Holland* TV show on which the band, with an extensive string section, finally convinced no small number of ageing cynics that they were more than just another bunch of anorak clad upstarts. 'Whatever', arguably the most Beatles-ish non-Beatles song ever written, proved that this was a band with soaring musical ambitions.

Apparently, Oasis were both flattered and appalled to hear that David Bowie, on hearing 'Whatever' and Liam's terrace chant "All the young blues, carry the news" on the intro, expressed a wish to see a song writing credit boasting Gallagher/Bowie. When challenged about this, Noel Gallagher sportingly announced: "Well he can fuck right off, can't he?"

*   *   *

For Oasis, the 1995 Brit Awards ceremony, in which they clasped the Best New Band category, was very much a rehearsal for the main event, their 'true' arrival, which would make the headlines from the same place, the same time, one year later. The 1995 ceremony, by stark contrast, would be very much the year of Blur who, despite being completely unknown to most people over thirty, waltzed merrily away with no less than four awards compared to one by Oasis.

It is perhaps worth noting that acrimony between the two bands was noticeably missing. Blur, looking as if they had just been plastering the walls, even shouted, "We think this should be shared with Oasis, love and respect to them." Oasis, who by contrast looked as if they had just returned from a hiking weekend in the Lake District, with Liam buttoned up to the neck, looked profoundly dismayed by the whole rigmarole.

Noel disgraced himself only by refusing to fall into his expected role of surly young curmudgeon, and flitted around the post-awards gathering, grasping startled artists and telling them, somewhat uncharacteristically, just how wonderful they were. He rectified this situation a few weeks later by admitting to Paul Mathur: "It was the E talking...I'd just like to say to all those bands, whoever they were, they are shit!"

On February 28, 1995, with memories of the ludicrous Brit Awards fading as fast as tabloid headlines, Liam Gallagher unwisely decided to test the strength of his celebrity by opting to go for a ordinary, old fashioned 'piss up' in Manchester town centre. The problem, of course, was that good old fashioned piss ups were no longer a option, once your face attracts attention from every quarter. Nevertheless, abetted by a mate, he bounced along to Oldham Street and, in particular, into the Factory/New Order owned Dry Bar, a cold stainless steel, marble and wood affair, famously attempting to fall in line with the surrounding redevelopment of the city centre's seediest area.

It is, even by New Order's admission, a strangely uncomfortable bar, offering no snug alcoves, no darkened corners at all and, rather like The Hacienda, favours lightness over dimmed intimacy. Despite being frequented by numerous pop luminaries, it offers no hideaways or unobtrusive recesses into which a famous face can retreat. Not that Liam Gallagher was in any mood for retreating. Or, at least, if he was, the barrage of gin and tonics that he waded through during a four hour binge served only to heighten the singer's precocity, and further demolish his already rather enfeebled sense of tact. He became, in short, a prat. At one stage, unable to contain himself, he began to insult a female customer. The girl's male companion, understandably taking exception, duly thumped Liam and an unsightly fracas ensued, during which glasses and ashtrays were dangerously hurled, though none actually hit anyone, tables were overturned and a chair allegedly smashed into the side of the bar (a chair which, it was alleged, was covered in Liam's vomit).

Finally, after much gentle force from Dry Bar manager Leroy Richardson, Gallagher and his friend were ejected from the bar, only to start a second fracas involving an indignant taxi driver.

Richardson subsequently informed the *Manchester Evening News* that "Liam and a mate had been in since three o'clock in the afternoon. It seems that the trouble started when Liam was rude to another customer's girlfriend and Liam's general attitude seemed to be that he was a pop star and could do whatever he liked. Well, not in this bar. We have a lot of very nice customers, but some of the most undesirable ones tend to be pop stars. This trouble came to a head when Liam broke a £70 vase and his mate tried to throw a table. Liam told me, 'I'm 'ard. I'm tough!' I had no choice but to throw them out."

Interestingly enough, when Creation were approached to comment on the incident, they claimed that it could not have happened because Oasis were elsewhere at the time and attributed the story to "people in Manchester jealous of someone who has got out". This fairly insulting reply was later ridiculed when Dry's general manager, Mark Sullivan, confirmed the rumpus had involved Liam. Sullivan stated: "I'm not sure if we have actually barred Liam, Leroy hasn't actually said that, although the bloke who hit him has been barred. We'll just have to see if he comes back and if he's all apologetic or if he still thinks he's above that kind of thing."

The silent friction between the band and drummer Tony McCarroll imploded softly during the spring of 1995. Local news stories suggested that McCarroll shuffled indignantly away from the limelight, apparently regretting nothing. His last appearance on an Oasis recording was on the major single 'Some Might Say' which provided a foretaste of the melodic shifts that would feature on the band's mighty second album.

McCarroll's replacement, Alan White, was introduced to the band by Paul Weller. Indeed, White's older brother, Steve White, has been a long serving Weller drummer, his services dating back to the early days of The Style Council. Joining Oasis on April 8, Alan White was first seen – much, surely, to the annoyance of McCarroll – in action as the band surged triumphantly into 'Some Might Say' on *Top Of The Pops*.

CHAPTER NINE
Blur vs Oasis:
A 'Needle' Match

The most tiresome media hype of the unusually scorching summer of 1995 was the so called Blur vs Oasis battle. It was a hype which began in the music press, more as a joke than an angle, which was plunged stupidly into the tabloids, where the South vs North angle was exploited with wearying effect. No record company seems prepared to take either blame or credit for it. It came into focus as the parallel singles, Blur's 'Country House' and Oasis' 'Roll With It', were steadying themselves for release on the same day.

The singles were quite the antithesis of each other. 'Roll With It' was, as ever with Oasis, a simplistic call to arms, a celebration, partly of being in a happening band and accepting the rollercoaster life that goes with it, and partly a statement of pure self-confidence. A few journalists noted that this was symbolic of Oasis' 'northern' arrogance although this was simply a ridiculous generalisation. 'Roll With It' is a wholly universal song with no specific 'northernness' about it at all. It was simply solid, uncompromising rock.

Blur's entry, 'Country House' – its very title reeking of pop star aloofness - was, on the other hand, heavily parodic and seemed positively featherweight by comparison. Noel's assertion that Blur were, "just middle class wankers twiddling about with fucking stupid sing-songs", probably didn't help dispel the row. What wasn't surprising was that Blur, with their solid college fan base and the instant pop nature of the single, would win this battle, and, sure enough, 'Country House' nudged above 'Roll With It' to the top slot.

The irony, of course, is that the pseudo English twee-ness of 'Country House' (which was very much a nod back to the

Kinks and which so effectively captured the attention of British radio) would ultimately condemn the band to relative failure in the USA, just like the Kinks themselves, at least during the sixties when they were at the height of their creative powers.

By stark contrast, the full rocking sound of what would surely become known as early period Oasis, did not suffer similar problems. Noel Gallagher knew this, full well, as he noted, "Well, we lost the battle, but there is no doubt that we'll win the war. They don't stand a chance, do they!"

A comedic, though profoundly anti-PC flare-up in the apparent Blur/Oasis war was presented to the press by Liam Gallagher as he unflinchingly launched into a verbal broadside in which he boasted of profound and lustful feelings towards Elastica's Justine Frischman who, naturally, happened to be romantically linked with Blur's Damon Albarn. The joke, if it was a joke, lasted several weeks, leaving Liam wholly undeterred after the comparatively eloquent Frischman had snubbed him at an awards ceremony.

"I was double rude to Justine the other night," he admitted soon afterwards. "going 'Go on and get your tits out'. It's her boyfriend innit, 'cos I love getting at 'im 'cos he's a dick. If anyone said that to my bird, I'd chin 'im. But I fancy her big style. I'm having her, man. In the next six months it will be all over the press, I'll have been with her. Don't say it, though, 'cos I'm mad for her and that'll screw it right up."

Two more – out of the many – outbursts from Liam would serve to emphasise the rather disrespectful force of this dubious lust. "I don't mind Elastica, they're alright. I'm into that bird Justine, yeah! I'm in love with that." And later, as if to re-activate the Blur vs Oasis war after the hype had mercifully calmed to a ripple, "they're a fucking mess, Blur are. They are the opposite from us. I mean, Elastica are better than them. I couldn't cope with that, me. No way would I allow my bird to be better than me, no way."

This distance between the two bands was duly emphasised by Blur's appearance on the BBC 2 Britpop special, also featuring Echobelly, Sleeper, Gene, Marion, Supergrass and Elastica. The programme, though rather entertaining, was sensibly avoided by Oasis, whose aversion to the term 'Britpop' had already been more than brusquely stated. For Blur's part, their light-hearted 'country gent' costumes, intended sarcastically, served only to accentuate their lightness. It was a strange programme, intended to solidify the strength and commercial power of Britpop. However, although the mighty Pulp saw no reason not to take their place in the line up, and certainly strengthened things by appearing, the entire thing formed a curiously dull mush. Bands like Echobelly, Sleeper and Supergrass, so refreshing when heard alongside East 17 and Boyzone on Radio 1, did seem to weaken considerably when placed back to back, despite the sexual allure that had been missing from the 'indie' generation that had preceded them.

Strangely and perhaps typically, the band that emerged with the most kudos from the whole caboodle, was Oasis, conspicuous by their absence.

CHAPTER TEN
What's The Story?
A Glorious Anti-climax

Being a hip, young, gun-slinging rock journalist must have been a mite confusing in September 1995. After all, what would you do if you were suddenly handed the second Oasis album, (*What's The Story) Morning Glory?* to review? Gosh what a difficult task! After all that had been written! For eighteen months, every loosely music based rag had been crammed solid with superlatives pertaining to Oasis. *Definitely Maybe* had all but swept the board and, gathered together, the reviews had gushed like Victoria Falls, collectively adding credence to the Gallagher brother's relentless braggadocio.

With this in mind, approaching the new Oasis album with a critical eye would be a nervy task. After all, however good the album, would the continuation of this mass praise be the correct thing to do, or would it be better to administer the odd critical slap? Was it time for a mini backlash? And, perhaps more significantly, would a writer's name be etched into rock journalism history by being the first to courageously slam Oasis? Or would he/she find themselves ridiculed/alienated? It was perhaps the ultimate test of a rock journalist's nerve.

Greatness or obscurity. It was twenty-two years since Nick Kent famously slagged the massively hip Pink Floyd because David Gilmour in live performance had greasy hair and split ends. This was of comparable gravity. Things at the *NME* and *Melody Maker* hadn't changed a bit.

The brothers had been telling the world for several months that the new album would be one of the all-time classics. Surely it wouldn't be surprising if this new batch of songs didn't quite live up to such immense expectations. Anything remotely short of genius could be immediately seized upon.

The critics took up arms, though they didn't exactly seem sure how to fire them.

In a sense, although Noel Gallagher would express a degree of confusion, if not hurt, the reviews proved curious. Though the album would in the end be universally praised, most of the reviews took one step back from positive torrents of words proclaiming Oasis the greatest thing on planet Earth. This reticence was enough to cause a huge sense of anti-climax within the band's ranks.

Perhaps a full-blooded backlash would have been far easier to accept. It would certainly have been more entertaining. However, the band, their confidence running into overdrive, hadn't expected the reviewers to pull back at all. And it was Noel Gallagher who arrested the band's sense of disappointment, by finally stating "Look, we knew how good it was when we made it...there's no reason why we should change our minds now...this record is going to take us straight to the top. This isn't a pretty good album...or an almost brilliant album...or a next step on the Oasis ladder album...this is a classic rock album. It will be up there, right at the very top...forever. So fuck them. Time will tell."

The irony, of course is that if any modern rock album deserved uncritical gush, to be praised to the heavens, then that record is (What's The Story) Morning Glory? It was a magnificent achievement, quite unparalleled and undeniably the album of the year, if not the decade. Paul Weller's Stanley Road, which featured Noel Gallagher picking his way uncertainly and acoustically through an absolutely blistering version of Dr John's voodoo-dope classic 'Walk On Gilded Splinters', has been perceptively referred to as a 'sister album' to Morning Glory. Weller would return the compliment by guesting on Morning Glory's soaring finale, the superb 'Champagne Supernova'.

This musical bonhomie, part and parcel of the Gallagher make up by now, reached ecstatic new heights during the day spent recording Go Discs 'HELP' album in September, the day on which Noel, much to his delight, became a member of rock's generally rather fickle hierarchy by meeting amongst others Paul McCartney. "From what I've heard from Paul McCartney, he likes about half a dozen of my songs," Noel said later. "I met him twice, on the *Come Together* album and then I went round his house in St John's Wood one night. He liked 'Slide Away', 'Whatever' and 'Live Forever'. If I'd been knocked over by a taxi that night, I'd have died the happiest man."

Morning Glory was, of course, stuffed with cliché. As if to emphasise this point, as if to proudly slam it into the listeners ears, the opening track, 'Hello', was an absurd nod towards glam rock, cheekily pitting Gary Glitter's most anthemic single, 'Hello, Hello, I'm Back Again', with Slade's power ballad 'Far, Far Away'. The 'steal', deliberately blatant, cast a rather joyous couldn't-give-a-toss-mate spell which would linger over the entire record.

'Hello' was followed by three huge Oasis singles, 'Roll With It', 'Wonderwall' and' Don't Look Back In Anger', so the game had been won before the fifth track, 'Hey Now', crashed with equal majesty from the speakers. The fact that many of the critics seemed to shy away from noting the record's state of simplistic perfection didn't matter at all. The fans would recognise it right from the very first chord in England, Europe, Japan and America. They had got the album that they had always wanted.

Noel Gallagher's songwriting had matured even if there still seemed little point in sifting through the lyrics, most of which, in true untaxing Oasis way, remained fairly meaningless. Even the great breakthrough single, 'Wonderwall', with all its bluesy intonations and irresistible hooks is a rather empty collection of Beatles references. It was also the title of George Harrison's first solo album, a largely experimental electronic record.

"It's always intentional," Noel Gallagher told *Sky* magazine. "I'm always trying to rip The Beatles off for anything and everything. People always say, 'Don't you want to be innovative?' Well, no. We just want to make good records. We always go for the obvious. People want to hear a song, then hum it, then wind it back, again and again."

The fact that this second collection of familiar licks, hooks, bridges, intros – who can resist the opening bars of 'Imagine' that sit on the nose of 'Don't Look Back In Anger? – proves gloriously entertaining shouldn't deflect from the fact that a portion of lyrics are worthy of scrutiny. The most obvious example is the John Lennon reference during 'Don't Look Back In Anger'. When Noel sang these lyrics several thousand sets of parents would mutter "That must be about John Lennon." Indeed, according to Noel, not only was it about John Lennon, it was practically written by him.

"I got this tape in America that had apparently been burgled from The Dakota (where Lennon lived) and someone had found these cassettes. Lennon was starting to record his memoirs on tape. He was going on about tryin' to start a revolution from his bed, and that people said the brains he had went to his head. Thank you, I'll take that!"

Such proud, honest thievery can only be admired. Some of the 'steals', however, did employ at least a small degree of subtlety. You have to dig pretty hard but, apparently, the Nirvana classic 'Smells Like Teen Spirit' lurks in the undertone of 'Wonderwall'. It also lurked beneath much of the first album. As Noel explained to *Sky* magazine: "People don't realise it but a lot of the first album comes from Kurt Cobain really. The way he wrote his melodies around his music I thought was genius. The first vocal line on any of his songs would always start low and then go up and up and then down, 'til the chorus, when he'd shout everything. But his melodies were very balanced. I think we are similar in the way we approach our melodies. 'Smells Like Teen Spirit' sounds like 'Wonderwall'. Very short words and melodies as well."

'Wonderwall' was the most 'singalong-able' single of 1995; joint top, perhaps, with Pulp's 'Common People'. It would be the song that not only broke the band on a global level but, more importantly in the minds of the Gallaghers, the song that finally cemented their status as Manchester City's top pop star fans. When it was suggested that 'Wonderwall' might even replace the standard Blues terrace anthem, 'Blue Moon', Noel Gallagher noted: "The Kippax sing the loudest, bestest songs 'cos we have more time to think them up waiting for City to put the fucking ball in the net...but for our song to be adopted by the Kippax would be the ultimate accolade for us...it doesn't get any better than that!"

*   *   *

Deep in the urban sprawl of Chadderton, hinged onto the edge of Oldham, 24-year-old bass guitarist Scott McLeod packed his instrument into his guitar case in preparation to join the rest of his embryonic band, Saint Jack, for their regular rehearsal session, when the phone rang.

For three years, Scott had performed, standing studiously stock-still in the manner of Bill Wyman, in the highly rated band The Ya Yas, co-managed by flamboyant ex-Stone Roses supremo, Gareth Evans, and he had seen all the usual disappointments and ego clashes that cloud the early careers of most bands. With Saint Jack, who had yet to perform live, he had helped to build a sound etched on the sound of The Byrds, The Beatles and The Rolling Stones. Despite these rather obvious influences, the amiable McLeod firmly believed that his band had found something unique.

The phone call changed everything. Oasis bass player Paul McGuigan was, in the words of his record label, suffering from "nervous exhaustion" and needed six months rest. Although Scott had known the Gallaghers from the days when The Ya Ya's rehearsed at The Boardwalk, he never in a million years expected that they would ask him to play the fill-in role. He had the weekend to tell the band, to steady himself, and to organise things before climbing on board a London-bound train, flanked by Liam and Bonehead, destined for two weeks intensive rehearsals before Oasis would depart for an all-important American tour. It was some responsibility.

Nevertheless, Scott rose to the occasion, performing with the band at New York, Baltimore, Pittsburgh and Boston before, on the eve of an all-important appearance on the David Letterman Show, he astonished and panicked the entire Oasis entourage by deciding to quit. Despite heavy pleadings from both the band and the tour organiser, Scott refused to remain with Oasis, and promptly flew back to England, leaving them with no option but to cancel the remainder of the tour.

The press that gathered around this odd story was full of tales of Scott's "homesickness" and inability to cope with the endlessly warring Gallaghers. The truth, he would later insist, was rather different. "At the end of the day, I found myself comparing the two bands and I preferred Saint Jack," he proclaimed, without a hint of irony. He continued, "Although I really enjoyed my spell with Oasis, I'm sure that Saint Jack will have their turn. I have no ill feelings against Oasis but I can't speak for how they feel".

The final poignant irony was, perhaps, reserved for Saint Jack's rehearsal room, as they ran through their set, one final time, before venturing out into a darkened, scarcely populated Manchester club to make their début. At precisely the same time that Oasis were readying themselves for two sell-out nights at London's Earls Court, on November 4 and 5, in front of an audience of 20,000, the largest crowd ever assembled for an indoor concert in Britain.

"Now that we have succeeded in there," stated an ecstatic Noel Gallagher after the second gig, "we can play anywhere. Nothing will ever top that."

"I now know I made the right decision," said Scott McLeod, following Saint Jack's inglorious, but nevertheless, promising live début.

*   *   *

The champagne, fittingly for once, had been flowing all night and at various times had been complemented by a variety of spirits and beers and wines. It was Creation Records' Christmas party and it was by far the most lavish party they had ever thrown, to celebrate the finest year, by far, in their relatively brief history. Prior to Oasis, the biggest band on their roster had been Primal Scream, who had swelled Alan McGee with pride by notching up over 500,000 album sales, a tasty amount for a fundamentally small band on a fundamentally small label.

Things had changed during 1995, though. Creation were no

longer a malicious upstart of a record label. At the time of the Christmas party, Oasis had nudged past 2.5 million album sales with *Definitely Maybe*, and when *(What's The Story) Morning Glory?* was unleashed on the States, it was certain, at the very least, to double that figure. Things could only get better and bigger.

Although the band's potential had been apparent to McGee from the very moment they walked on that Glasgow stage at King Tuts, and that Noel Gallagher's songwriting had continued to astonish him again and again, there had still been a small niggling doubt, things can always go wrong, especially with such a volatile band. But, by December 22, 1995, all kinds of barriers had been broken. The world had simply opened before them. Creation, and Oasis, had truly arrived.

The bash took place at the Halcyon Hotel in Holland Park in west London. It was little different to any other record company party taking place in the capital that week, being a mess of haughty backslapping and simmering sexual tension. On the stroke of midnight, however, the atmosphere altered. Calling for silence, McGee rose to his feet as everyone readied themselves for the usual 'end of term' banter. This time, perhaps, a mite more congratulatory than usual.

To everyone's surprise, he called Oasis drummer Alan White over to him. White, somewhat abashed, was handed a gift wrapped box. Stunned, he opened it to discover a model of a toy Mini Cooper S, complete with famous Union Jack roof. Looking pleased with his new toy, he duly ripped open the card to discover a cheque, large enough to cover the cost of a real Mini Cooper S. Astonished, for he hadn't even been a band member for long, he staggered back to his seat, wondering if the whole thing might collapse into some kind of prank. It didn't. Bonehead, equally surprised, was next up and for his pains he was presented with a Rolex watch. While still gloating over this, he ripped his card from the envelope to read that, back in his living room, a new piano lay waiting for him. 'Guigsy' also received a Rolex, plus membership to a posh gym, while Liam's surprise package included a Rolex, a bundle of clothes and a new Epiphone guitar, a copy of one used by John Lennon.

Such extravagance, of course, caused a certain amount of tension in the room. What, most people were now thinking, would be the big one. What would he give Noel?

Escorting the songwriter to the hotel window, he pointed to a chocolate coloured vintage Rolls Royce. The story would appear in the *NME*, adorn the tabloids and scream from Radio 1's *Newsbeat* the next day.

"Well, what am I going to do with it?" asked Noel Gallagher, "I can't drive."

CHAPTER ELEVEN
Odds, Sods, Brits & Brats

The car, at least as far as the press was concerned, made its début at the Hard Rock Cafe on January 25, when Noel Gallagher attended the launch of what would, three and a half weeks later, become a tumultuous Brits Awards Ceremony. As the band had been nominated for five Brits, Gallagher had agreed to speak to the assembled 'hack pack'.

Much to Gallagher's surprise, the event turned into an unholy scramble as pressmen struggled to catch a quote. Perhaps for the first time in his life, as his chocolate brown Rolls Royce whisked him through the streets of central London, back to his Camden Town apartment, Noel Gallagher truly began to feel like a genuine pop star.

With the help of a driver, more necessity than affectation, although Gallagher would stress that, "real pop stars don't drive, they are driven" he would bring the car, once again, into the glare of the press spotlight on January 23, when he attended the parodic annual *NME* Brat Awards. Accompanied by his girlfriend Meg Mathews, he wouldn't need to side-step any tabloid frenzy – they were readying themselves for the Brits – and, as the only member of the band in attendance, he sullenly scooped up four awards alone. Well, almost alone, as manager Marcus Russell was never too far away from his arm. No emotion creased his features as he sat, as impassive as a Buddha, while the ceremony proceeded. Finally, as Vic Reeves called his name, he sidled wearily to the stage, completely ignoring Reeves, who seemed rather lightweight and superfluous and spat into the microphone, "It's hard to be humble at times like these, so I won't try. You're all shit!" Even this seemed to merit applause, and he returned to his table, proudly clutching his four trophies.

Later, holding court, arrogance dripping from his shoulders, and with the worst of the tabloid "idiots" at bay, he decided he wanted to chat. Immediately, everyone shuffled respectfully into position before him. *NME, Radio 1, Shift, Ozone, The Big Breakfast, Manchester Evening News* and it was a reporter from an Irish radio station who risked death by asking about the tiresome Blur vs Oasis rivalry.

"We lost the battle but won the war," said Noel. "I always said that we would. It's not a quick sprint. We know how good we are, there are people who love our band, we know how good they think we are. We don't have to prove anything to ourselves, least of all a load of journalists. "

Nevertheless, this particular 'load of journalists' asked if the band felt justified at receiving four awards from the readers of the *NME*.

"Of course we do. We all feel justified. There was this stuff round the time of 'Roll With It', people were writing us off and saying this was the first knock back and we were finished and all that. But we know how good our records are, we know how good the band is and we know how good musicians we are. And I know how good a songwriter I am, so I don't have to justify ourselves to anybody except the people."

Relaxing into a state of supreme confidence, Gallagher continued to answer every question in a manner of outrageously positive self-appraisal. One could only admire him even if, at times, his gloating became rather testing for those who were paid to listen. That stated, who could seriously begrudge him this triumph. What a year it had been. *Morning Glory* had risen to No.9 in the USA – and was bound for No.1 – and it was cemented to the No.1 spot in England. The single, 'Wonderwall', similarly, had been languishing in superior chart positions for a full thirteen weeks (and the Mike Flowers Pops cover version, hanging onto the overblown easy listening boom, had only just missed the Christmas No.1 spot).

More than this, Oasis were truly mesmerised by the American industry machine. As they flitted around London and Manchester, they knew that, out there in Seattle, in Chicago, Los Angeles and New York, their music was a living, breathing organism, swelling, encroaching into all kinds of areas, turning the heads of the kids, slipping into households and screaming from a thousand radio stations, rippling across the States, on MTV, on beatboxes. It was out there and almost impossible to control.

Noel Gallagher: "We are just sitting back and watching this thing from across the Atlantic, thinking 'What the fuck is happening?' You know, because I don't know what it is. Over here we can judge what we do and see what kind of people are getting into it...I have no fucking idea who is listening to us in America. But, it's weird, if you took a kid from the Bronx and a kid from Brixton who probably have nothing in common whatsoever, the one thing they would have in common is that they would both own a copy of *Morning Glory*. That's something to be proud of, and we are. When we came here last year, and it was all Blur and Oasis, and we were saying, 'We are the best band in the world and we are going to be the biggest band in the world', and everyone was, like, 'Go back to Manchester and keep you gobs shut'. And now we are getting there, man, we are on our way."

*   *   *

Meanwhile, back in Manchester, as Noel Gallagher was asserting his self-confidence, fans of the band were arriving from across the country, feverishly scrambling, and often failing, to secure tickets for a much touted Oasis gig at the band's beloved Maine Road on April 28. City, away to Aston Villa that day, would be hoping that the Oasis show would be a celebratory event, with the team having avoided the drop into the First Division. As tickets went on sale, however, the team's position seemed perilous, and would worsen during the following month.

It took just 24 hours for all 39,000 tickets to fly from the agent's booths, fuelling speculation that the band would be playing a second date, though Oasis' management swiftly denied this.

Wallowing in his new London base, Noel Gallagher was

often to be seen, with Meg Mathews faithfully by his side, wandering through the West End, nosing through the music shops in Denmark Street. He was engaged in his favourite activity – browsing among guitars – on Thursday February 16, when the area, shaken by the impending threat of a renewed IRA bombing campaign, was completely sealed off following the discovery of a 'suspect device' 200 yards away.

Much to the consternation of Meg and, indeed, to customers similarly trapped in the shop, the police announced that nobody could leave, and that the imprisonment could possibly last for a couple of hours. In the end, it was three hours before the doors were reopened. The imprisonment did have its compensations though, for Noel Gallagher, resigned to three hours of tedium, seized the day by grasping one of his favourite guitars and running through a variety of Oasis hits followed by a lengthy trawl through an array of rock classics. Falling happily into the spirit of the occasion, the disgruntled punters joined in with Noel, turning the dreary afternoon into the most unlikely singalong.

In February 1996, the British pop industry's orgy of self congratulation, The Brit Awards, steadied itself in readiness for Oasis sweeping the board, in much the same manner as Blur had the previous year. There was a little pre-ceremony banter with the band resolutely refusing to perform live. "We wanna enjoy ourselves and get pissed, we don't wanna work," stated Noel Gallagher, punkily, to the *Manchester Evening News*, and few people could blame him.

Oasis scooped three awards – Best Single for 'Wonderwall', Best Video and Best Band – and to no-one's surprise proved to be profoundly ungracious recipients. At a post-ceremony press conference, Noel Gallagher sneeringly concluded, "We didn't sweep the board. We didn't win the lot, we only won three when we should have won six...only the award for the best video – voted for by the fans – means anything to us. Awards voted for by corporate idiots in pony tails mean nothing to us." This would probably have made the front pages had Pulp's Jarvis Cocker not leapt on to the stage to protest against Michael Jackson assuming the role of God and found himself in police custody for his trouble.

The Oasis display seemed like a welcome show of solidarity between band and fans, but a petty streak of wholly predictable 'laddishness' marred the ceremony. Apparently still hurting from their previous year's trouncing by Blur, Oasis fell into a impromptu tongue-in-cheek version of 'Park Life' re-written as 'Shite Life'. There was nothing too shocking about that but later, on receiving an award from INXS singer Michael Hutchence, Liam Gallagher duly announced, "Michael's going to give me a slap round the face...so come on!" The can of Red Stripe may have accounted for this. Then Noel said: "I have nothing to say except I am extremely rich and you aren't...and has-beens shouldn't present fucking awards to going-to-be's," a remark which endeared him to absolutely nobody. More encouraging perhaps, was Noel's assertion that there were seven people in the room who were giving a little hope to young people in this country...himself, 'our kid', the rest of the band, his record company manager and Tony Blair.

But there was more to it than that and there was certainly more to it than appeared on the famously sanitised TV broadcast, a one and a half hour travesty which bore little resemblance to the actual event. Naturally, the next morning, the tabloid headlines were filled with Jarvis and Liam's shock horrors. Later that week the *NME* would refer to the programme as a 'televisual lie' and this writer, in dutiful attendance, can only share that sense of indignation. In truth, the drama had begun weeks before the ceremony when Noel stated publicly that he "didn't feel like working on the night," and turned down the opportunity to perform live.

This caused a severe problem for the Brits organisers, especially as it became obvious that Oasis would easily win the Best Band category. The banter between Liam Gallagher and Hutchence, puerile as it was, was grounded in the fact that Hutchence had recently been photographed with Patsy Kensit – Liam's date on the night – whose hand was down the front of his trousers. There were other factors too. Hutchence, rather stupidly, and probably incorrectly, had stated in the *NME* that his new solo work would "piss all over Oasis."

But, in terms of PR, Noel Gallagher – simultaneously a PR dream and PR nightmare – gave two glorious press conferences during the evening of the Brits, before and after, his every word deliciously slicing into the heart of the British music establishment. But his 'bite the hand that feeds' mentality caused very little consternation, for his every utterance would simply sell more records, and thus feed the industry he so despised.

Reporter: "Noel, I'm from *The Big Breakfast*. Can you tell me what 'Shite Life' was all about?

Noel: "It's called Marmite...(sings) Marmite...(pointing to the questioner) You look like you were in Bros. Were you in Bros?"

TV Presenter: "Now that Take That have split up, do you think it's the end of manufactured boy bands?"

Noel: "Are you taking the piss?" (Though, actually, it was a rather good question).

Reporter: "Noel...I'm Simon London, *Live TV*. What did you think of the Manchester derby match? (during which Man Utd had beaten City courtesy of a disputed penalty).

Noel: "Right, well, we'll say to that referee, if you are watching, the 'lads' are on your case and you are gonna get your fucking windows put in." (This, he later admitted, wasn't a joke).

The Net on Radio 1: "Which of the three awards is most important to you?"

Noel. "None of them. They are all voted for by idiots in pony tails with dicky bows."

The Net: "But one was voted for by the fans." (The Video award, by *Chart Show* viewers).

Noel: "The one that's voted for by the fans means a lot. Anything that's voted for by fans is special. Anything that's voted for by fans means a lot. Anything that's voted for by idiots, by corporate pigs, means nothing to us."

Terry Christian: "What do you think of the sixth round of the FA Cup?"

Noel: "Shut Up."

Christian: "What can you teach America about Brit Pop?"

Noel: "We are not part of Brit Pop."

Perhaps funnier were the words he spat into an *NME* tape recorder during the ceremony: "We need the people of England who are on the dole, unemployed and buy the records, to tell us how good we are. That's all that matters. I feel satisfaction that people buy the records, of course, but we are the best band and we did record the best album. It's as simple as that. It's not like we are walking around, crowing about it. (Not much)."

"Why is someone like some fucking weather girl and all the other tossers presenting fucking awards? (Good point). Michael Hutchence! What's he doing presenting me with an award? You should have had Johnny Marr up there. You should have had Keith Richards. Paul McCartney. What's a fucking weather girl got to do with awards and British music? That's what's wrong with British music, man. The only people I have respect for are Jarvis, Black Grape, Supergrass...I've got a lot of respect for Cast. And what is Michael Jackson doing here, apart from to further his own career? That's crass, man. That fat idiot from Simply Red. What's he doing with 650,000 dancers on stage? Do me a fucking favour. What about fucking Bjork? And PJ Harvey? Annie Lennox? What's she done? Ever, in her entire life? Ever, ever, ever, ever? Let alone this fucking year."

"We'll come here, get pissed, and take the awards. But I tell you what, man, they're fucking presented by idiots...My band doesn't need some corporate fat pig who earns £450,000 a year and wears a dicky bow and thinks Sting and Phil Collins are the cutting edge of music to tell me how good my fucking group is. They can stick their awards and stick them right up their country houses."

CHAPTER TWELVE
America Falls – March '96

The failure of the British bands of the nineties to successfully surge into the main arterial flow of the American music industry, or even to break through on a smaller, cultish level, had been puzzling the English rock hierarchy since the demise of Madchester. Indeed, the problem had even surfaced in broadsheet financial pages and, in 1993, in a couple of earnest reports in British television arts programmes. Time and time again a wave of carefully constructed hype would be followed by a British band's mini-tour of selected live shows that prised only lukewarm reactions from American audiences.

The Americans weren't impressed by the sight of some fey, callow youth cavorting in front of three denim clad devotees to 'student anti-chic', punching their way through a maze of dated Bowie and Velvet Underground riffs. The problem was most famously highlighted by the astonishing failure of Suede while their support band, The Cranberries, surfed all the way onto the cover of *Rolling Stone*. Indeed, *Rolling Stone* proved a fairly accurate indicator to the limited damage inflicted by British acts. Bands would regularly flicker and die on its pages, more often than not cast aside after attaining the obligatory half page feature as 'new British hopefuls'. The failure of the Stone Roses, who seemingly had the world at their feet at the start of the decade, was a case in point. They preferred to sit in their Welsh farmhouses, drink beer and play with their children than spend time conquering state after state. Fair enough, one might reasonably conclude, but the fact is that the Stone Roses looked every inch a world dominating act, more than capable of following in the footsteps of U2. And in the end they delivered...nothing. The difference, of course, is that U2 – and The Cranberries – were prepared to work hard.

Even Britain's biggest adult pop band, Simply Red had become rather embarrassingly the largest album selling act in the world, bar America, where their status seemed to be receding, year by year.

That stated, there had been a few notable breakthroughs. No one can doubt the strange, though probably fleeting success of Take That, Seal and Everything But The Girl, of Bush and Eternal, and of smart little acts like Elastica, Portishead and Supergrass who filtered onto a college circuit that preferred Inspiral Carpets to the legions of dour sub-Nirvanas nurtured in America's vast suburbia. Nevertheless, it was a ripple rather than a wave, individual flashes rather than an invasion.

It would surely take a band of awesome magnitude and talent and audacity to finally smash down the barrier. Could this band be Oasis? After all, with the Stone Roses pointlessly side-lined, they had seized the thunder on this side of the Atlantic and there was something universal about their material, it could easily reverberate around the large US stadiums, as U2's music had done a decade earlier.

It could be done although, even as late as February 1996, Blur's Damon foolishly noted, "the only similarity between us and Oasis is that we both mean zilch in America." Ouch! Two weeks later (What's The Story) Morning Glory? crashed into the US album charts at No.4. The world was beginning to listen. Suddenly, 100,000 Americans were purchasing the album every seven days. This was 'big time' and, in the context of the nineties, it was breaking new ground.

Typically, no great master plan had preceded this breakthrough, other than Noel Gallagher's usual brash confidence. "Of course we will break America," Noel had stated in mid 1995, "because we are brilliant, the songs are brilliant and brilliant songs are universal." No doubt this, and similar outbursts in the British press, had caused considerable ripples of muffled laughter in the management offices of some of their rivals.

The Stateside story had begun back in 1993, the ink barely dry on the band's Creation contract, when Alan McGee and Marcus Russell met David Massey, head of A&R at Epic

Records in the States and bashed out a world-wide deal with (again) alarming ease. Massey had seen the band at The Powerhaus in London in 1993 and, as he explained to *Q* magazine: "Liam was bundled up in a coat that went up to his chin and he was wearing tinted glasses. You could hardly see him but there was something extraordinary there. It was at a time when UK bands were as cold as ice in the US and there was some cynicism in the company when we signed them – but we were already convinced."

The most marvellous irony here, of course, is that Liam's image, far from being contrived, was – the sun-glassed affectation aside – lifted directly from the streets of Burnage. Place him on those pavements, or in the sullen masses who flocked to Maine Road every other Saturday, and this apparent charisma would instantly melt. Again, unwittingly, Oasis had turned heads in a completely natural manner. Massey, actually an Englishman who had, until catching Oasis, shared the Epic corporate apathy about English acts, had been "blown away" by simple street chic, be it Gio Goi, Joe Bloggs or Manchester City football strips.

Richard Griffiths, head of Epic, was similarly convinced. "They (Oasis) have reaped their rewards by making it clear that they are pro stardom. They unashamedly want to be successful at a time when a lot of American bands have been deliberately doing what they can to try and limit their success and be very much the anti-hero. The Gallaghers have shaken the Americans up a bit – and they get away with it because they are incredible."

Indeed, Oasis had been introduced to America in the spring of 1995 with the comparatively low key release of *Definitely Maybe*. Wisely, the company, knowing that a second album would be ready for release within a year, kept the album bubbling while the band, reluctantly, worked their way through a network of grubby clubs. After modest success with both the album (sales of 2.5 million) and the single, 'Live Forever' (500,0000), the major breakthrough came with the rocky 'Morning Glory' single and, of course, 'Wonderwall'. With the *Morning Glory* album pushing past the five million sales barrier, and showing little sign of levelling, and with the American arena circuit beckoning loudly, a swift graduation into the 'super-stadiums' seemed inevitable.

The US breakthrough was deemed so important that the *NME*, traditionally the paper that plans the backlash once the band have become too big to guarantee (or have any need for their record company to provide) freebie flights for journalists and photographers, decided to dedicate a full page of quotes on Oasis in the US, mostly congratulatory, from assorted British bands – hiding their envy, no doubt – and pop luminaries. Most interesting, perhaps, was Alan McGee's delight-fuelled rhetoric.

"Oasis are the best British band since The Clash. Everyone goes on about the bands that failed in the eighties. But they weren't good enough, at the end of the day. And the ones that were good enough weren't prepared to work hard enough. They were releasing an album every three or four years, like the Stone Roses, and America isn't really interested in that. Oasis have gone to America six times in two years and that's how they have done it. The turning point was 'Wonderwall'. It's Noel's songs. Liam's voice. Liam's sex appeal, the right management, and the right record label. They've got the lot. The album has sold four million and I predict it will sell 12 million. In time they will be the biggest band in the world. They are No.1 in Italy, Israel, Australia and England. I never knew they'd be this big when I signed them. They are the most professional band. If Liam can't sing, Noel will sing and then they'll go back and play the gig again. Their management is totally professional and so are the band. If they decide to do something, they do it properly. They are the biggest thing since Nirvana."

Meanwhile, back in Britain, Oasis' very fine rivals Blur and Pulp could merely sit and watch. Could America ever, similarly, clasp their comparatively British songwriting streaks with such fervour? It seemed doubtful. Noel Gallagher, by religiously sticking to tried and tested rock clichés, was not selling America anything remotely unsteadying or unfamiliar. The US audiences could accept it with ease; after all, both

Oasis albums are littered with familiarity. By contrast, what on Earth would they make of Jarvis Cocker?

Whatever, the Oasis train seems to move on and on, with the band pledging that in 1996 they will release no new records, but simply promote *Morning Glory* on a global scale. But for a songwriter of Noel Gallagher's stunning prolificacy, a problem has already arisen. Once a band hits the very top of the pile, alongside Simply Red, U2 or R.E.M., the industry cogs slow to a crawl and there is no demand for fresh work each year. Indeed, if the industry has its way, Oasis would already have fallen into a four year cycle. The problem is that, quite rightly, there is no way that Noel Gallagher can stem the flow at this point. It seems almost certain, at the time of writing, that he will take the band back into the studios for lengthy sessions during the course of 1996. His American bosses may not like it, but with apparently twenty new songs already burning to be recorded, and with his head swilling with more and more, his desperation to trap them on vinyl while still fresh will certainly defy any long term record company strategy.

"I'm afraid of running dry," he says, "every songwriter is afraid of picking up a guitar and nothing coming out. That's why we keep going. Your most recent song could be your last. You might as well keep it fucking good. I'm going to record four albums before I lose the point unlike, say, Lee Mavers of The La's who only did one...and the Stone Roses, we learned a lot from them. They didn't do anything for five years and a lot of record company people were actually applauding that inactivity. There is pressure on us to slow down...but I don't think I can do it. I think back to what The Beatles did in that eight year period. All that music. In today's climate they would only have been asked for two or three albums."

Oasis are certain to break through that conventional slowing down, even if it is to their eventual commercial detriment, though they might just manage to precociously shame the 'laziness' of big scale rock acts, simply by continually swamping the charts on both sides of the Atlantic and that, certainly, hasn't been achieved by any English band since...well, who do you think?

"Whenever I start feeling good about myself," Noel told *Sky* magazine's Ken Micaliff, "I just think of The Beatles' albums and those eight years and I know I ain't that fucking good. Not yet. But I will be that good. I think that anyone in a band should have the ambition to be as good as these guys (The Beatles). You have to be blessed with the talent. You can develop it to a certain extent, but it has to be there. Maybe one day I'll write a song better than 'Something'. Maybe I already have. It's not for me to say. But it's definitely within me grasp. We've got it in us to be the biggest band on the planet, bar none. We believe in ourselves just like The Beatles."

Endpiece

Having conquered America, most of Europe, much of Japan...having sold eight million albums...having won three Brit Awards and, more to the point, having supplied 'chant' material for Maine Road's Kippax End is not enough, it seems, to tear the family away from its staunch Burnage roots.

Although, as these words are being written, both Noel and Liam are attempting to prize Peggy from her modest social circle and, good naturedly, install her in a mansion in Southern Ireland, both brothers would surely regret this move. Life will never be the same again for the Gallaghers. As it is, March 1996 sees the family, still sadly split, still straddling the odd divide between modest domesticity and a glittering superstar lifestyle. Not since George Best resolutely refused to leave his Chorlton-Cum-Hardy landlady in the sixties has such a wrench been so apparent.

And no more apparent than on Mother's Day, Sunday March 17 1996, when Liam, fresh from the band's truly ground-breaking US tour, turned up, flowers in hand, at his mum's Burnage semi. This somewhat touching scene harboured, also, an equally touching matriarchal outburst from Peggy. For, the very next day, tabloid diarists filled their columns with heady reports of a split between Liam and Patsy Kensit.

According to one report, the couple had split following a 'bust up' over Patsy's still close relationship with former husband, Simple Minds singer Jim Kerr. The story continued with a false account of Liam rushing to London in an attempt to patch things up with Patsy. As it happened, nothing of the sort took place. Liam put his feet up, and telephoned Patsy from the family sofa.

Peggy, reading the reports the next day, seemed incredulous. "Is this what always happens when people become famous?" she asked naïvely, "because it makes me really angry.

Everything between them is fine and as far as I know, always has been. The rumours are just not true...I wish the papers would leave them alone. They are two young people who should be left to get on with things for themselves."

Alas, such days are over. Part of the price, it seems, one has to pay for being a member of the finest band on the planet. Twenty-four hours later, Liam was standing on a stage in Cardiff, screaming 'Roll With It' in front of a packed, intense, frenzied audience. He had spent his day in an insular, irritable huff, fending off reporters, snapping at photographers.

Peggy, by severe contrast, had probably wandered to the newsagents, stopping off, along the way at the local café, for a fag, a cup of tea and a chat.

OASIS

DISCOGRAPHY

Singles

(Titles in bold designate main releases)

Columbia (demo)
Creation CTP 008 (12" one-sided promo, 510 only, black die-cut sleeve) December 1993

Supersonic
Creation CRE 176 TP (12") April 1994

Supersonic/Take Me Away
Creation CRE 176 (7") April 1994

Supersonic/Take Me Away/I Will Believe (live)
Creation CRE 176T (12") April 1994

Supersonic/Take Me Away/I Will Believe (Live)/
Columbia (white label demo)
Creation CRESCD 176 (CD) April 1994

Shakermaker/D'Yer Wanne Be A Spaceman?/
Alive (8 track demo)/Bring It On Down (Live)
Creation CRESCD 182 P (CD) June 1994

Shakermaker/D'Yer Wanne Be A Spaceman?
Creation CRE 182 (7") June 1994

Shakermaker/D'Yer Wanne Be A Spaceman?/
Alive (8 track demo)
Creation CRE 182T (12") June 1994

Shakermaker/D'Yer Wanne Be A Spaceman?
Creation CRECS 182 (cassette) June 1994

Shakermaker/D'Yer Wanne Be A Spaceman?/
Alive (8 track demo)/Bring It On Down (Live)
Creation CRESCD 182T (CD) June 1994

Live Forever
Creation CRE 185 TP (12") August 1994

Live Forever/Up In The Sky (Acoustic)/Cloudburst/
Supersonic (Live)
CRESCD 185 P (CD) August 1994

Live Forever/Up In The Sky (Acoustic)
CRE 185 (7" limited edition, numbered foldover p/s, in
poly bag) August 1994

Live Forever/Up In The Sky (Acoustic)/Cloudburst
CRE 185T (12") August 1994

Live Forever/Up In The Sky (Acoustic)
CRECS 185 (cassette) August 1994

Live Forever/Up In The Sky (Acoustic)/Cloudburst/
Supersonic (Live)
CRESCD 185 (CD) August 1994

I Am The Walrus (live)
Creation CTP 190TP (12" promo, Live at Glasgow
Cathouse, June 94, 250 only) October 1994

Cigarettes And Alcohol
Creation CRE 190TP (12" promo, 300 only) October 1994

Cigarettes And Alcohol/I Am The Walrus (Live at
Glasgow Cathouse, June 94)
Creation CRE 190 (7" limited edition, numbered foldover
p/s, in poly bag) October 1994

Cigarettes And Alcohol/I Am The Walrus (Live at
Glasgow Cathouse, June 94)/Fade Away
Creation CRE190T (12") October 1994

Cigarettes And Alcohol/I Am The Walrus (Live at
Glasgow Cathouse, June 94)
Creation CRECS 190 (cassette, flip top 'cigarette' pack)
October 1994

Cigarettes And Alcohol/I Am The Walrus (Live at
Glasgow Cathouse, June 94)/Fade Away/Listen Up
Creation CRESCD 190 (CD) October 1994

Cigarettes And Alcohol/I Am The Walrus/Listen
Up/Fade Away
Creation CRESCD 190P (CD) October 1994

Whatever
Creation CRE 195 TP (12" one sided promo, 560 copies)
December 1994

(It's Good) To Be Free
Creation CRE CTP 195 TP (12" one sided promo, 360
copies) December 1994

Whatever/(It's Good) To Be Free
Creation CRE 195 (7", numbered foldover p/s, in poly
bag) December 1994

Whatever/(It's Good) To Be Free/Slide Away
Creation CRE 195T (12") December 1994

Whatever/(It's Good)To Be Free
Creation CRECS 195 (cassette) December 1994

Whatever/(It's Good) To Be Free/Slide Away/Half The
World Away
Creation CRESCD 195 (CD) December 1994

Slide Away
Creation CCD 169 (CD, One track, 1000 only, Brits promo,
unique card sleeve) March 1995

Some Might Say
Creation CCD 204 (one track promo CD, 350 only)
March 1995

Some Might Say/Talk Tonight/Acquiesce/Headshrinker
Creation CRESCD 204P (CD promo) March 1995

Some Might Say/Talk Tonight
Creation CRE 204 (7", foldover p/s, in poly bag) March 1995

Some Might Say/Talk Tonight/Acquiesce
Creation CRE12T 204 (12") March 1995

Some Might Say/Talk Tonight
Creation CRECS 204 (cassette) March 1995

Some Might Say/Talk Tonight/Acquiesce/Headshrinker
Creation CRESCD 204 (CD) March 1995

Acquiesce
Creation CTP 204 (12" one-sided promo, 570 only)
April 1995

Acquiesce
Creation CCD 204P (promo CD, one track only, 300 only)
April 1995

Roll With It/It's Better People/Rockin' Chair/Live
Forever (Live at Glastonbury 1995)
Creation CRESCD 212P (promo CD, 3078 only,)
August 1995

Roll With It
Creation CTP212 (12" one-sided only) August 1995

Roll With It/It's Better People
Creation CRE 212 (7", foldover p/s, in poly bag)
August 1995

Roll With It/It's Better People/Rockin' Chair
Creation CRE 212T (12") August 1995

Roll With It/It's Better People
Creation CRECS 212 (cassette) August 1995

Roll With It/It's Better People/Rockin' Chair/Live
Forever (Live at Glastonbury 1995)
Creation CRESCD 212 (CD) August 1995

Round Are Way
Creation CTP 215 (12" 843 only) October 1995

Wonderwall/Round Are Way/The Swamp Song/The Masterplan
Creation CREDSCD 215P (CD, 2320 only) October 1995

Wonderwall/Round Are Way
Creation CRE 215 (7", foldover p/s, in poly bag)
October 1995

Wonderwall/Round Are Way/The Swamp Song
Creation CRE 215 T (12") October 1995

Wonderwall/Round Are Way
Creation CRECS 215 (cassette) October 1995

Wonderwall/Round Are Way/The Swamp
Song(Live)/The Masterplan
Creation CREDSCD 215 (CD) October 1995

Cum On Feel The Noize/Champagne Supernova
(Lynchmob Beats Mix)
Creation CTP 221X (12", 1203 only) February 1996

Cum On Feel The Noize
Creation CCD 221 (picture CD, one track, with football
motif) February 1996

Don't Look Back In Anger/Step Out
Creation CRE 221 (7", foldover p/s, in poly bag)
February 1996

Don't Look Back In Anger/Step Out/Underneath The Sky
Creation CRE 221 T ((12") February 1996

Don't Look Back In Anger/Step Out
Creation CRECS 221 (cassette) February 1996

Don't Look Back In Anger/Step Out/Underneath The
Sky/Cum On Feel The Noize Creation CRESCD 221 (CD)
February 1996

Albums

(Titles in bold designate main releases)

LIVE DEMONSTRATION
Cloudburst/Strange Thing/D'Yer Wanna Be A
Spaceman/Columbia/Bring It On Down/Married With
Children/Fade Away/Rock 'n' Roll Star
(Cassette only, limited edition of tracks recorded at the
Real People studio in Liverpool in mid 1993) 1993

DEFINITELY MAYBE
Rock 'n' Roll Star/Shakermaker/Live Forever/Up In The
Sky/Columbia/ Supersonic/Bring It On
Down/Cigarettes And Alcohol/Digsy's Dinner/Slide
Away/Married With Children
Creation CRE CD 169 (CD) August 1994

(Double album vinyl version (CRE LP 169) includes extra
track, 'Sad Song'; also cassette (CRECS 169))

OASIS LIVE
Rock 'n' Roll Star/Columbia/Fade Away/Digsy's
Dinner/Shakermaker/Live Forever/Bring It On
Down/Cigarettes And Alcohol/Married With
Children/Supersonic/I Am The Walrus
Creation (promo only) February 1995.

(WHAT'S THE STORY) MORNING GLORY?
Hello/Roll With It/Wonderwall/Don't Look Back In
Anger/Hey Now/Some Might Say/Cast No
Shadow/She's Electric/Morning Glory/Champagne
Supernova
Creation CRED CD 189 (CD) October 1995

(also on vinyl CRE LP 189 includes extra track
'Bonehead's Bank Holiday' and cassette CRECS 189)

(WHAT'S THE STORY) MORNING GLORY?
Creation CRE CD 189 P (CD, withdrawn, black card
sleeve, includes extra track 'Step Out') October 1995

(WHAT'S THE STORY) MORNING GLORY?
Creation CCRE 189 P (cassette, withdrawn, black card
sleeve, includes extra track 'Step Out') October 1995

(WHAT'S THE STORY) MORNING GLORY?
Creation CCRE CD 189 P (CD, 7650 only, black card
sleeve) October 1995

(WHAT'S THE STORY) MORNING GLORY?
Creation CCRE 189 P (cassette, black cover, 500 only)
September 1995

Miscellaneous

WIBBLING RIVALRY
Fierce Panda NING12 (12" interview disc of taped
conversations between Noel and Liam, 1000 only, later
repressed on CD: NING CD and 7": NING7 with barcode
on sleeve) November 1995

MUTHA OF CREATION
Cigarettes And Alcohol (demo)
NME CRE 10 (Various artists compilation cassette given
away with *NME* magazine) February 1994

SECRET TRACKS 2
Fade Away (demo)
Select Tracks 2 (Various artists compilation cassette given
away with *Select* magazine) May 1994

HELP!
Fade Away/Come Together (credited to
Smokin' Mojo Filters)
Go Discs LP 828-6821 and CD 828 6822 (Various artists
compilation) September 1995

K-VOX BLASTING THE AIRWAVES - THE TODD
ROGERS SHOW
Bring It On Down (Live)
VOX GIVIT 6 (Various artists compilation cassette given
away with *Vox* magazine) October 1994

CLASS OF 94
Rock 'n' Roll Star
Vox Givit 9 (Various artists compilation cassette given
away with *Vox* magazine) December 1994

REALLY FREE
Slide Away
Q/Our Price Q99 CD (Various artists CD compilation
given away with *Q* magazine) December 1994

THE WHITE ROOM ALBUM
It's Good To be Free (Oasis)/Talk Tonight
(Noel Gallagher & Paul Weller)
Q No cat. no. (cassette) (Various artists compilation given
away free with *Q* magazine) February 1996

NME SINGLES OF THE WEEK 94
Supersonic
RCA 7432163752 (CD)
January 1995

BRAT PACK '95
It's Good To Be Free
NME BRAT (cassette, free with *NME* 28/1/95)
January 1995

COMING DOWN
Shakermaker
Creation CRE CD 135 (CD compilation)
1995

CREATION UNRELEASED
Acquiesce
Sony SAMP 2821 (CD sampler, card sleeve)
March 1995

104.9
Married With Children (Live)
XFM CD 2 (CD, taken from 'Live By The Sea' Cliff's
Pavilion gig)
October 1995

BRAT PACK '96
Bonehead's Bank Holiday
NME BRAT 96 (cassette, given away free
with *NME* 27/1/96)
January 1996

WHAT'S THE STORY?
VOX DOC 96 (cassette, Radio 1 documentary from
3/9/95, given away free with *Vox* 5/96)

Video

LIVE BY THE SEA
PMI MVN 4914773 August 1995

CD Video

LIVE BY THE SEA
Polygram 914772 March 1996

US Promo's

Live Forever (3.49)/Live Forever (LP version)
Epic ESK 6435 (CD, silk screened sleeve) August 1994

Supersonic (Edit)/Supersonic
Epic ESK 6464 (picture CD) January 1995

Rock 'n' Roll Star (Edit)/Rock 'n' Roll Star
Epic ESK 7024 (picture CD) January 1995

(What's The Story) Morning Glory? (Edit)/(What's The
Story) Morning Glory? (LP version)
Epic ESK 7302 (picture CD) November 1995

Champagne Supernova (Edit)/Champagne Supernova
Epic ESK 7719 (CD) 1995

Wonderwall
Epic ESK 7440 (picture CD, custom sleeve)
November 1995

(What's The Story) Morning Glory?
Epic ESK 7361 (CD, unique sleeve showing the back of
Noel's head) October 1995

Live In Chicago
Epic ESK 6705 (CD) 1995

European Rarities
(French except last entry)

Sad Song/Cloudburst
Sony SAMP 2347 (CD, in 'Definitely Maybe' style sleeve)
1994

Singles Collection
Sony HES 661111-2 (5 CD box set, 4000 only, including
Supersonic/Shakermaker/Live Forever (with extra track
Live Forever (Edit)/Cigarettes And Alcohol, plus a 4 track
live CD 'Live Footage')
February 1995

Definitely Maybe
Sony SAMP 369 (2 CD, with bonus disc featuring
Whatever/Supersonic)
August 1994

Acquiesce (Live)/It's Good To Be Free (Live)
Sony HES 4810209 (promo CD)
1995

Definitely Maybe
Sony CRESCD 169 P (CD, 5 track promo sampler, blue
card sleeve)
August 1994

Japanese Rarities

Definitely Maybe
Sony ESC A-6045 (CD, with 2 extra tracks
Cloudburst/Sad Song)
1994

Some Might Say
Sony ESC A-6251 (CD single, 2 extra tracks Some Might
Say (Demo)/You've Got To Hide Your Love)
1995

Australian Rarities

Definitely Maybe
Sony SAMP 369 (2 CD, with bonus disc featuring
Whatever single)
August 1996

(What's The Story) Morning Glory?
Sony No cat. no (2 CD, with extra disc featuring
Cigarettes And Alcohol)
October 1995

(What's The Story) Morning Glory?/It's Better
People/Rockin' Chair/Live Forever
Sony 662488-2 (CD, B side tracks live at Glastonbury '95)
October 1995

Also Available

Laser Discs: Oasis feature on over thirty laser discs, which are largely used for karaoke machines, but are also widely available to the Japanese public.

Also worthy of note is the rare Oasis Red Double Decker Bus, a solid die-cast toy, with 'Morning Glory' livery.

INDEPENDENT MUSIC PRESS

BRITAIN'S LEADING ALTERNATIVE MUSIC PUBLISHER

THE EIGHT LEGGED ATOMIC DUSTBIN WILL EAT ITSELF

The first and only detailed account of Stourbridge's finest, including previously unpublished photographs, exclusive interviews, a complete discography and reviewography, and an introduction by Clint Poppie. *Vox* described the début book and it's success as "phenomenal".

160pgs with 38 photo's £6.99 + £1p+p

THE MISSION: NAMES ARE FOR TOMBSTONES, BABY

The official and fully authorised biography of one of the UK's biggest goth bands. *Melody Maker* said "This makes Hammer of the Gods look like a Cliff Richard biog!", *The Times* praised the "impressively detailed research" whilst *Record Collector* hailed "a tight fluid book which pulls no punches with an enviable degree of confidence, all utterly compelling stuff."

288pgs with 38 photo's £6.99 + £1p+p

THE RIGHT TO IMAGINATION AND MADNESS

With an Introduction by John Peel
This landmark book provides lengthy interviews with 20 of the UK's top alternative songwriters including Johnny Marr, Ian McCulloch, Billy Bragg, Prodigy, Boo Radleys, The The, Pwei, MC4, Napalm Death, Wedding Present, Senseless Things, Utah Saints, BTTP, Aphex Twin, McNabb, Ride.

450pgs with 35 photo's £9.99 + £1.25 p+p

MEGA CITY FOUR: TALL STORIES & CREEPY CRAWLIES

This authorised biography is a comprehensive study of of this seminal band, containing 40 photographs taken from the band's own album, over 30 hours of interviews and a complete discography. *NME* said "its attention to detail is stunning", *Q* magazine said "the incredible detail is breathtaking", whilst *Record Collector* hailed it as "a valuable account, true drama."

208pgs with 40 photo's £6.99 + £1.00 p+p

THE PRODIGY - ELECTRONIC PUNKS

The official history of the world's most successful hard dance band, including hours of exclusive interviews with band members, families and friends, as well as photographs taken almost entirely from the band's own personal albums. *Electronic Punks* is IMP's biggest selling title and moved *NME* to call Martin Roach "the biographer of the indie heartland."

160pgs with 38 photo's £5.99 + £1p+p

THE BUZZCOCKS - THE COMPLETE HISTORY

The fully authorised biography of one of the prime movers of the original punk scene. Author Tony McGartland recounts in stunning detail every gig, rehearsal, tour, record release and studio session the band ever played, and reveals rare unpublished photo's. *Record Collector* said "this book is invaluable", *Vox* called it "a bible for Buzzcocks fans" whilst *Q* declared it to be "an exhaustive documentation of these punk pop perfecto's that only prime mover Pete Shelley could possibly improve upon."

160pgs with 25 photo's £8.95 + £1.25p+p

POP BOOK NUMBER ONE - STEVE GULLICK

This fine collection of Steve Gullick's work from 1988-1995 captures the key figures in alternative world music. With rare and unpublished shots of Nirvana, Pearl Jam, Hole, Blur, Bjork, and many more, this is the most accomplished photo history of alternative music. *The Times* called it "one of the most beautiful and necessary books about 1990's pop and rock" whilst *Melody Maker* said "So stylish, so rockin'."

112pgs with 108 duo-tone photo's £12.95 + £1.50p+p   SOLD OUT

DIARY OF A ROCK 'N' ROLL STAR - IAN HUNTER

Widely regarded as the first rock autobiography and universally acclaimed as one of the finest ever insights into life on the road, this best-selling title is now re-printed for the first time in 15 years. Revealing the rigours of Mott The Hoople's enigmatic frontman, this is a landmark publication. *Q* magazine simply called it "the greatest music book ever written."

160pgs with 28 photo's £7.95 + £1.00p+p

PLEASE MAKE CHEQUES/POSTAL ORDERS, INTERNATIONAL MONEY
ORDERS PAYABLE TO: *INDEPENDENT MUSIC PRESS*

AND SEND YOUR PAYMENTS TO: INDEPENDENT MUSIC PRESS,
P.O.BOX 3616, BETHNAL GREEN, LONDON E2 9LN
Please allow 30 days for delivery

YOU CAN ALSO ORDER VIA THE INTERNET:
http://www.rise.co.uk/imp